LYRIC LINE

Equestrian Fiction by Barbara Morgenroth

Bittersweet Farm 1: Mounted
Bittersweet Farm 2: Joyful Spirit
Bittersweet Farm 3: Wingspread
Bittersweet Farm 4: Counterpoint
Bittersweet Farm 5: Calling All Comets
Bittersweet Farm 6: Kyff
Bittersweet Farm 7: Lyric Line
Bittersweet Farm 8: Tea Biscuit
Bittersweet Farm 9: Roll the Dice

If Wishes Were Horses ~ a novella

Middle-grade

Dream Horse
Summer Horse

~ BITTERSWEET FARM 7 ~

LYRIC LINE

Barbara Morgenroth

DashingBooks

Bittersweet Farm 7: Lyric Line © 2014
Barbara Morgenroth
http://barbaramorgenroth.com

ISBN: 978-0692325193

Cover photo by Bob Haarmans
Published by DashingBooks
Text set in Adobe Garamond

1

"TALIA! WE'VE GOT A PROBLEM," Greer called.

I lay my forehead against CB's shoulder. There had been problems since early morning, starting with a thrown shoe and the assurance that the farrier couldn't get to the farm until the end of the week. All I wanted to do was get on and ride into the woods before the freezing rain started. "Hang on," I told him and went to the entrance.

The commercial horse transport drove into the yard and stopped at the barn.

"Who is that?"

"I don't know," Greer replied and started toward the two men in the process of letting down the ramp.

Following her outside, I watched as the trailer rocked from side to side, there was the sound of scrambling hoofs, and then a large horse dragged one of the men down the ramp. He snorted as the second man grabbed his halter.

"Where do you want him?"

"Minnesota." Greer replied. "Who did this?"

"Two guys sent him from Hialeah. Where do you want him? We got other horses to deliver before the weather craps out on us."

I looked at Greer. "A race horse?"

"What are we going to do with a race horse?"

The stallion whirled around nearly knocking one man down.

"Lower barn," Greer said. "I don't care which one had this bright idea, they're both getting yelled at." She started for the barn and the men followed her.

Cap Rydell stepped closer to me. "Turn him out. Bring him in around May."

I laughed knowing she was semi-serious. "Have you ever had a horse straight off the track?"

"No, have you?"

I pointed to Butch standing at the fence with the ponies. "That was my transportation before CB."

"Bijou," Cap reminded me of her sweet hunter. "As far as the barn Mill and I had, race horses don't make good polo ponies. They're too tall. Mill would have no use for a horse like this."

We went back into the barn together and I finished tacking CB. Just as I was about to unclip the cross ties, my phone started ringing.

After looking, I clicked it on. "Hi."

"I guess the horse arrived already."

"Yes, how did you know?"

"Cam is on the phone. I assume by his expression that Greer is giving him hell."

"Where are you?"

"On Roux," Lockie said, "and in line waiting to ride the Citrus Classic course."

"Why'd you send us a stallion? He practically tore the trailer apart and snorted like a steam engine all the way to the barn."

"We got him at Hialeah, cheap. Deep Stack's a nice horse."

Deep Stack? What kind of name was that?

We had different definitions of nice. I thought a horse was nice if it didn't take two people to act as tug boats and navigate the thing to where you wanted to go.

"He's not fast enough for the track."

"And?"

"You know what happens to young horses that can't win."

"Please, Lockie! Don't do that to me."

I knew very well what happened in situations like that and didn't want to think about it. I also didn't know that

3

we could manage this horse. There were ponies and little girls in that barn who thought every horse pooped glitter and didn't understand some weren't pets.

"I have to go, Tal, my number was just called," he said. "Are you mad at me?"

"No. Good luck. Be careful. And come home." The last thing Lockie needed was to go into a jumper class with his attention elsewhere.

I clicked off and rubbed CB's ear. "I don't know where you came from but I'm grateful someone treated you well."

He stuck his nose against my face and exhaled on me. I blew a breath into his nose then led him outside so we could have our hack before the weather turned mean on us.

***

Greer sat down to dinner.

"I thought you weren't going to talk to Cam anymore," I said.

"I wasn't talking, I was screaming at him."

"What happened," Jules asked.

"They sent us—"

"The spawn from hell," Greer finished for me. "We'll be lucky if he doesn't destroy the stall overnight. Fortunately, there are no mares in the new barn."

There was silence for a moment.

"It seems cold in here to me," I said. "Should we turn the thermostat up?"

Greer ignored me. "It's a horse that's too much for any of us to handle. It's not just deeply quirky like Kyff, who will be fine after six months of psychiatric counseling."

Jules looked up from her Chicken Francese. "Tell me about your foalhood, Kyff. Did you feel the absence of your father terribly? How was it being raised by a single mother?"

I pressed my lips tightly together so I wouldn't smile. There was no benefit to upsetting Greer more than she was already. Besides the fact that I agreed with her. There was no one on the property who had experience with a horse like that.

"That's not funny!"

"I'm sorry, Greer," Jules said.

Greer pushed back from the table, leaving dinner unfinished and slapped her hand against her thigh. Joly, our puppy, followed her from the room.

"Was it insensitive of me?" Jules asked.

With my lips unpressed, I could laugh. "No. I think it's a number of things. The horse arrived unannounced. His name is Deep Stack. I have no idea what that means."

"It's a gambling term referring to the stack a chips a player has," Jules explained.

"Thank you. It would have been good if we had been consulted about him first. The stud's unexpected arrival was an unnecessary upset."

"For Greer?"

I nodded. "She's still so angry with Cam for his misstep in Florida. And she'll never forgive her mother."

"Has she forgiven your father?"

Looking down the length of the table to the empty chair, then to Lockie's empty chair next to me, I nodded. "I think so. She never mentions it. When is she upset by anything and doesn't mention it?"

"That's true."

"She's right about this horse, I think. I hope he's sold without us doing anything with him."

"Didn't Lockie tell you what the plan was?"

"No, he was thirty seconds away from entering the ring. I haven't heard from him since. I hope he finished the round safely."

"Wasn't it on the Internet?"

"It's not possible to find the results for every class. Maybe later."

Of course, if there had been any real problem, Cam would have called. I was grateful he was there and knew he would keep an eye out on Lockie for me. Whether Cam was a good judge of what I'd consider a danger or not was entirely another issue.

Jules got up from the table and returned with dessert. "What are you going to do about that horse?"

I shook my head. The young stud horse was a pointed message that we didn't know very much. We knew how to ride a trained horse, but we didn't know how to train a horse. CB babysat me. I was the student. He was the instructor. Greer could do whatever she was told, and was so good at that. But neither of us could start at zero and begin to work with a horse who only knew two speeds—prance in place and flat-out gallop. Lockie had come to the farm for a reason. We needed a trainer.

As Jules and I finished dessert then cleaned up after dinner, I wondered how we were going to get through the entire month of February with Lockie and Cam in Florida sending us horses to deal with. Maybe it would be wise to suggest they hold off for a couple more weeks. I didn't mind the idea of another horse or two being at the farm to relax for a few days until Lockie came home for good but not for weeks.

Being in Florida and riding for Teche Chartier's Acadiana Farm was very good for Lockie and by extension Bittersweet Farm. He was picking up his career when he had left off some years ago and people were noticing him as well as his success in the ring. That meant we were also getting noticed.

I knew he felt comfortable with where he was. We didn't talk about it a great deal because he was well aware that I would prefer it if he was home and training horses rather than competing at speed over very large fences. This was true. I was concerned about his well-being but that wasn't a negative. I was concerned about everyone in my family. If pressed, I would even say concerns existed for Cam but there didn't seem to be much reason for it.

***

I was just saying goodnight to CB when my phone rang.

"Hi."

"Why didn't you call me?"

"Why didn't you call me?" I offered CB the last piece of carrot in my pocket.

"We went to a business dinner with Teche. I was hoping you'd call and get me out of it."

"How do you feel?"

"Tell me again that you and Greer are not sharing emotional states."

"I'm not angry but I'm baffled. Why didn't you call to tell us?"

"The truth?" Lockie asked.

"Yes, it's the best place to start."

"I forgot."

8

This was magnitudes worse than having a colt dropped off in the yard.

"Don't worry about me," Lockie insisted.

I took a breath. "Then I'm not sorry Greer yelled at Cam because he has no excuse."

"Don't blame him. He thought I called."

After his accident with Wing on the cross-country course a few years ago, it was not unusual for Lockie to have small lapses in memory, but this was the most significant one I knew of. To-do lists were backups but he probably thought he didn't need to be reminded to call me since we spoke several times a day.

We had spoken yesterday and he didn't mention the horse. Lockie had once told me it was like throwing a rock into the pond. It didn't leave a hole. There was nothing to tell him he was forgetting something. The memory just wasn't made.

I shut off the lights for the barn and walked to my truck. "Is there any possibility you can go to the doctor in Palm Beach Dr. Jarosz recommended?"

"I'm okay but if it will make you feel better, I will."

"Thank you."

"You knew I would if you asked me, Silly."

I did. "Call and make the appointment and let me know when it is so I can remind you."

Lockie laughed. "I'll talk to you tomorrow. Or call me to remind me to call you."

At least one of us found this humorous and it obviously wasn't going to be me.

***

When I got back to the house, Greer and Jules were watching an old movie on television.

"And I'm accused of making bad choices? No one in history has made the stupid decisions that this chick has," Greer said pointing at the screen as I entered the room.

Jules patted her on the leg. "No one would suggest you don't consider all elements of a situation before you act irrationally, Greer."

"Thank you for that totally backhanded compliment I will cherish for the next thirty seconds."

"Sit down and watch with us," Jules said to me.

"This day has been too long. I'm going to get into bed. May I borrow Joly for a while, Greer?"

She nodded.

***

My day wasn't over. Ten minutes after Joly and I settled down for the night my phone rang.

This time I recognized it as Ryan Saunders, the twelve year old with the three hundred thousand dollar pony.

"Hi, Ryan."

"Hi, Talia. I just got back from Florida."

What kind of schedule was this kid on?

"How did you and Ding do?"

"Lockie and Cam helped me, so we won the large pony hunter but Isla O'Hara took the equitation."

As far as I was concerned, that was no great loss but she was disappointed. "There's always next time," I said.

"Instead of me spending my winter break in Florida can I come to the farm and ride with you?"

My mind stopped working for a moment I was so surprised by this suggestion. Almost any coach would be a better choice than me, even if was only based on the fact that they liked showing. I still found little to recommend standing around waiting for classes all day in what was usually some sort of bad weather.

Fortunately, my out came to me. "Your pony is in Florida. Will you want to take lessons on other ponies not your own?"

I loved my ponies but they didn't cost more than a Volkswagen let alone a Lamborghini. There was a reason Sideshow Ding cost as much as he did. He was the Superboy of ponies.

"I'll have him brought north."

"Do you have a barn for him now?" I was trying to follow along and was failing.

"I'll send him to Bittersweet," Ryan replied. "You have room, don't you? Counterpoint's stall is empty."

"Yes, we have some empty stalls but I have to be honest. You need a better coach than me. You need someone who has experience in the pony division. I never showed in ponies. By the time I started riding, I was already too tall for anything but a horse."

"But you showed your horse on the A circuit."

Under duress. "Yes, I did."

I put my hand on Joly's back. His coat was like silk velvet and the color of blue steel. He opened his eyes and looked at me with such compassion, I felt humbled. How was it possible to be that young and to understand humans so completely?

"It's just for a week."

"Fine. You can bring your pony here for a week. During that week, you will ride and we will also find you a new coach."

"Talia," Ryan began to protest.

Greer entered my bedroom and sat on the edge of my bed.

"You need someone closer to your school. My sister knows the area, I'm sure she'll have some suggestions. That's your choice."

"Okay." Ryan sighed. "I'll call you when we make the arrangements to ship him to you."

"Good girl. Now go to bed. This is too late for you to be awake. Bye."

"Bye."

Greer looked at me. "Who was that and what area do I know?"

"Ryan Saunders. New York State. We need to find her a coach closer to her school. I feel sorry for the kid. She's got no one. The father doesn't give a damn and the mother is in Paris. Her last coach was that Moron guy."

"Moran?"

"Whatever."

"He's a mean bastard but he produces winners."

"The holy grail of everything in life," I replied.

"Winning is not a character flaw," Greer said.

"Needing to win..." I realized how this was coming out. "I didn't mean you."

"You're right. I thought I needed to win. Ryan thinks she needs to win to get her parents' attention. She's probably right. They will praise her for five minutes and go back to ignoring her." Greer paused. "Not giving your best effort to everything you do isn't an effective means of protest, Tal."

Had I done exactly what Ryan was doing but in reverse? Was my own failure the only way I could punish my father for the loss of my mother? Was it my attempt to keep him out of my life? If I didn't succeed at anything he pushed on me, wasn't that a very small and bitter triumph?

"You're right. We're so screwed up."

Greer shook her head. "It's in the past. Make the best of any situation, bad or good. Tell me about this kid and her pony."

"Sideshow Ding is one of those miniature Thoroughbred ponies that is so typey, so cute, it leaves you weak in the knees."

"And the problem is?"

"She needs a coach who believes in the showing, the equitation, the competition as if it has meaning."

Greer stretched out across the bottom of the mattress.

"We did it all wrong, Greer. We were both miserable but for different reasons. I don't want to get into that same loop again. If I take some ponies on, I want showing to be a small fraction of their equestrian education. In my world, no one can learn enough over the five or six days between shows to have competing every weekend make sense."

"Why can't Ryan be in your program?"

"Her school is in New York. Is she going to commute here every day after school? Then what's she going to do with this pony? Dress it up for Valentine's Day as a pink cupcake with a heart quarter mark?"

"Are you going to have the Zuckerlumpens do that?"

"No, but they will, and find heart shaped sequins to glue on their ponies' hoofs."

14

"If they're going to do that, seriously, let's use them for Ambassadors of Good Cheer."

I considered it for a moment. "If the girls are going to put the glitter on them anyway, could we have a pony parade in town? We could invite the 4-H club to participate. They could circle the green and prizes could be given for fun categories. We could use the sayings that come on the heart candies. Gallant Guy. Sweet Tweets. I know there's not much time but you're so good at organizing things, Greer."

She nodded and stood. "We'll need a permit if we're going to block traffic for ten minutes. I'll call the Town Hall tomorrow. Keep Joly for the night. He's good company."

"Thank you." I stroked his head. "Yes, he is."

2

THE NEXT MORNING we looped the lead shank over Deep Stack's nose and got him outside with almost no trouble. He ran up the hill bucking the entire way as Cap and I watched him go.

"We can look forward to getting him back in, if we can catch him," I said as we returned to the barn.

"I'm telling you, that issue is solved if you leave him out for the next two months."

We both laughed, then I came back to reality. "He won't still be here in two months."

Cap looked at me. "You hope."

Greer grabbed my arm as I stepped into the barn. "Come on, we're going to town."

"I was going to ride CB," I protested.

"Ride him later."

I was dragged to my truck. "Why can't we go in your truck?"

Greer gave me one of her looks.

"Am I supposed to figure it out? It's a beautiful truck. The roads are dry for a change. What?"

She got in the passenger side.

"Are you going to tell me that you're never going to drive the lovely present you got for your birthday because Cam touched it last?" I started the engine.

"I will eventually drive it," Greer replied.

"Are we talking about months or years?"

"Not years."

"Good news." At the top of the driveway, I turned left. "Where are we going?"

"Park near the Town Hall. We'll do all our errands, then we'll go to the Feed Store so we can drop off the rest of these flyers." She waved a large envelop at me.

I found a parking spot near the Town Hall but sufficiently away from Rowe on Main Antiques in case Victoria might see us. The town clerk gave us permission to hold our rather impromptu parade but we got a lecture on taking the police away from their important work in order to stop traffic for us. Greer handed her a set of flyers and posters.

We stopped at the Grill Girl and asked if they would put a poster in the window. They thought that would be terrific if it was possible for them to sponsor one of the awards so people would come to the restaurant for a taste of their new double fried fries. Greer suggested they set up a table on the green, give out samples and a coupon.

It was difficult to believe how quickly she came up with these promotional ideas and I could only hope it wouldn't snow on Valentine's Day. Shoveled paths to French Fries covered in snowflakes instead of salt were conditions unlikely to bring many customers to the restaurant.

The hardware store was our next stop to request a poster in their window. They said yes. Within a half hour, we had Main Street covered with posters and flyers.

The feed store was our last visit and we headed home.

As soon as I drove toward the barn, I knew something was wrong. Deep Stack was not in the field and the immediate explanation was that he jumped out. It was a good sized fence but not impossible for anyone to clear if they were determined. I hoped he was smart enough to stay on the property because I didn't want to call the police away from their important jobs like giving people tickets for coming to a rolling stop at the stop sign, and instead drive around in their patrol cars looking for a horse running wild with his tail up.

"He's out. How are we going to find him?" I asked.

"You'll get on CB. I'll get on Keynote. Cap can get on Bij and we'll do the cowboy routine."

I pulled the truck up in front of the barn. "Here's the next problem. What happens when we find that monster?"

"Try to think positively, Tal. Maybe he'll follow us home," Greer replied. "We'll carry some grain in a bucket."

Getting out of the truck, I tried to imagine Deep Six, er...Stack, following CB docilely back to the barn. What if he attacked us, kicking at CB thinking a fight was necessary to stake out territory as the alpha horse? Who else was available to ride? Someone fitted for protective armor, preferably.

I stepped into the barn and met up with Pavel. "Everyone is in indoor," he said and went back to realigning a stall door.

Greer looked at me. "Who is everyone?"

"Cap and Freddi. It's too early for the Zuckerlumpen." This was what we called the pony riders, my version of German for sugar lumps because they were so sweet.

"Let's drag them away from whatever they're doing and find the stud horse then have lunch."

"If we can't find Deep Six, we're not eating."

"I'm not skipping lunch because of him," Greer replied as we stepped into the arena.

And came to a dead halt.

Lockie was in the middle of the ring and Cam was riding Deep Stack on the rail. Cap and Freddi were in a corner staying out of the way.

Instead of throwing serial bucks, the stallion was trotting quite calmly and Cam wasn't struggling with him in the least. From a distance and seeing him under tack, he was a beautiful horse, although thinner than anyone else on the property.

Cam trotted past us. "Good morning, Miss Swope."

"I'm going up to the house," she said to me, and left.

Stunned by their unexpected arrival, I walked to the center of the arena and put my arms around Lockie.

"You were right, Silly," he said into my ear. "I did need to come home."

I buried my head in his shoulder and he held me tight.

"It's okay."

I shook my head unable to speak.

"Yes, it is."

"How many hours are you going to be here?"

He stroked his hand over my hair. "I go back for the weekend and I'll be here on Monday."

"I don't understand."

"I'm commuting."

Cam stopped Deep Stack next to us. "Then I don't have to hear 'What do you think Talia's doing?' fifteen times a day. He misses you. If he can't say the words, I can."

"Is this a barnyard version of *Cyrano de Bergerac*?" I asked.

"I would hope we're a bit more sophisticated than that," Cam replied and turned the stallion back to the track.

"If Cam has anything to do with it, soon I won't have any secrets," Lockie said.

"You have secrets?" I asked.

"Everyone does," Cam called to us. "It makes us fascinating and dangerous." He urged the colt into a canter.

"You're staying home?" I asked Lockie.

"I promised Teche I'd finish WEF for him. It's only for a few weeks and he doesn't have a problem flying me back and forth. Counterpoint can finish up the last few shows, get the experience and exposure as we planned and at the end of the month, we're done. I'll be back here underfoot."

That meant during the week in Florida, the responsibility to exercise and train the horses Lockie was riding probably fell to Cam. We owed him again. Or I did. Greer would certainly not tolerate owing Cam so much as a used and sticky candy wrapper.

Lockie eased his hold on me. "What don't you like about this horse?"

Cam reined the colt into a walk then halted and dismounted.

I sighed and gestured with my hands trying to explain it.

"He's so big and so..." I looked to Cap for help.

"So..."

"Is this a word game? Um. For ten points...manly?" Cam replied. "Masculine? Studdish?"

"He dragged two men to the barn," Cap said.

"The pony riders. They don't understand..." I started.

"How did you turn him out this morning?"

"We thought about carrying a bucket of grain in front of him," Freddi said.

21

Lockie gave me a squeeze. "I'm sorry. It never occurred to either of us that you'd never been around a big colt."

"We have. Big colt geldings," Cap replied sharply.

Cam laughed. "Yeah, the gelding part makes all the difference."

"I'm sure stallions can be very civilized," I said. "But McStudly didn't look like one of those."

"We wouldn't send you something unmanageable." Lockie went to the horse and removed the saddle. "Cap come here and start cooling him out."

She didn't move.

Lockie led the colt to her. "He'll be fine. You did the video on how to lead a pony. Same thing. If he starts to pick up speed, what do you do?"

"Run in the opposite direction." Cap asked, straight-faced.

Cam laughed.

"Treat him just like any other horse. Pay attention. Give him a little tug on the reins. Give him rules." Lockie held out the reins. "He's got a bit in his mouth. He understands that."

"Rules. Gotcha." Cam left the arena carrying his saddle.

We watched as Cap led the colt around the arena without incident.

"What about with a halter and no bit," Freddi asked.

"What if there's a mare in heat?"

"Exactly!" Cap called from across the ring.

"Ladies. Think about it. There were fillies at the track. There were mares at the barn. He wasn't a maniac."

Cap stopped and looked at Lockie. "Then what transformed him in the trailer from Gentleman Jim in Florida to a fire-breathing dragon when he got here?"

"He's a young horse who just traveled fifteen hundred miles. Cut him some slack."

"None of us have been around a horse like him," I said in our defense. "It was a sh...surprise."

"I understand that. We're here to learn. All of us," Lockie replied and started to leave the indoor. "When he's cool, bring him into the barn."

***

An hour later, McStudly, the name fit him, was in his stall eating his lunch and we were up at the house eating ours. We, minus Greer. She had gone to visit the leader of the 4-H Horse Club to finalize some of the arrangements concerning their participation in the Valentine's Day parade.

The timing wasn't odd. She wanted to avoid Cam and did. He ate and went to back to the barn to ride Jetzt. Instead of this being a happy day, there was an undercurrent of tension partially due to Greer and Cam, and partially because we had gotten off on the wrong hoof with McStudly.

After lunch, Lockie asked me to manage the barn while he lay down for a while. With the Zuckerlumpens due to arrive for their lesson, there wasn't much I could do but stay at the barn while wanting to go to the carriage house and at the very least, make sure he was comfortable.

There were times when I felt as though something I couldn't define had come between us. Perhaps it was physical pain, perhaps it was the misfiring of neurons seeking pathways that no longer existed, perhaps it was my own clumsiness. Some situations could not be fixed and it was necessary to seek repair by other means.

Going to CB, I took care of him instead of Lockie, trying to repay him for all he gave me and knowing I wasn't even coming close.

Later in the afternoon, very predictably, Poppy and Gincy discovered the colt in the barn when they went to get their ponies. I felt that a combination lock was required on his door so that they wouldn't sneak in and try to braid streamers into his tail. To them, a stallion was something they had met in books or on TV, proud and brave, neck arched, tail cascading behind him and who possessed an eerie mindreading ability with the only person who could ride him. Reality for the Zuckerlumpens were their ponies who would put up with little girls crawling around under their bellies and pretending their tails were fright wigs.

24

These were things a horse fresh off the racetrack would not understand.

"We have two events this month." I guided them away from McStudly's stall before they could put buckets on the aisle to stand on for a better look inside. "There is a Valentine's Day Parade around the town green."

"YAY!"

"And we have a show."

Grabbing onto each other, they jumped up and down.

"Obviously Valentine's Day is the 14th but the parade will be the Saturday before. Think about what you would like to wear and how you might present Beau and Tango."

"Are we allowed to do anything we want?" Gincy asked.

"Within reason," I replied.

"RED GLITTER HOOF POLISH!" They cried at the same time.

"Don't embarrass yourselves or your ponies." Remarkably, I didn't add "wear nothing that identifies you with Bittersweet Farm".

"Tail bows with hearts on them!"

"Bridle charms!"

"Very creative," I said, wondering how badly this idea could go wrong. How many girls were in the 4-H Club? That times two.

Note to self: hire someone for the day to chase down loose ponies running around town stepping on their reins.

"Tack your ponies and meet me in the indoor for your lesson. You also have a show this month and you want to be ready for it."

"YAY!"

"How many classes can we enter?"

"You may enter one division. Pony Hunters," I replied.

Smiley faces turned into frowny faces.

"Feel free to go without me and enter as many classes as you'd like."

"Talia," Poppy protested. "I don't want to go without you."

"Thank you, that's very sweet of you to say. So cheer up, we'll go, and you need to tack your ponies for the lesson."

"After the lesson, can we pet the new horse?"

"No, you may not. I mean it."

When I was a child, before Butch even, my mother had listened to my begging long enough and one weekend in the country, we went to a stable to visit the horses. One horse had been confused thinking I had a treat and my entire arm up to the elbow went into his mouth before I knew what was happening. Luckily, he didn't bite down. Poppy and Gincy could pet McStudly if he proved himself to be an upstanding citizen but not before.

Cam was riding Jetzt in the indoor when I arrived.

"Time for your pony riders? I'll clear out in a minute," he said.

"Don't rush. It's good for them to learn about traffic."

He began cantering. "You want your horse to be above the ground," he said to me. "If your horse is going downhill, heavy on the forehand, it's not in balance. Everything becomes more difficult."

I watched him ride for a minute, studying him carefully. If Lockie was elegant, Cam was a power rider. They were built differently but beyond that, it was more the sense I got from each of them. The style was similar, both were classic and quiet in the saddle. Each movement was calibrated. Just enough, never too much.

"I'm sorry Greer is being so scratchy," I said as Jetzt began walking.

"No apologies are needed."

I started then stopped as the search for an explanation began. "I was going to say she wasn't raised to be discourteous but actually I have no idea how she was raised. Sometimes it seems like the Kensington-Rowes were a pack of wolves, not minor royalty."

Cam smiled.

"You know what her mother is like. Victoria is...awful."

"I've met so much worse," he replied. "My father worked with an actress, one might be generous and say she was in the descendancy of her career. My brother and I had small parts in this movie so we were able to see an ultra-diva in action."

"I hope she didn't proposition you," I said.

"We were just children. I was very cute, though. I looked like my father. I still do but my hair isn't as blond as it once was."

"It's pretty light now."

He removed his helmet and ran his fingers through his hair. "Did the sun bleach it?"

I nodded.

"Everyone says I look better as a blond."

Poppy and Gincy entered the ring and Cam dismounted close to me.

"Don't worry about Greer." He ran up his irons.

"How can I not?"

"You have to trust her. Hey, girls. Have a good lesson."

"Us?" Gincy asked.

"You." Cam left the ring.

"Talia. He noticed us. Cam Rafferty!" Poppy pretended to faint on Tango's back.

***

With the afternoon chores completed, I got in my truck and started up the driveway. There was a light on in the carriage house. I stopped the truck for a moment halfway between the two. Was he awake or did he just leave a light on downstairs? Did he want company or did he want to be alone? Was he all right or did he need help?

I drove straight and parked next to his truck. At the door, I knocked then opened it. "Lockie?"

"Hi, Tal, come sit with me."

I shut the door behind me and went to the sofa. It was a little cold in the room and there was no fire. "Would you like me to turn up the heat?"

"No, this is fine."

He patted the cushion next to him and I sat down.

"Have you eaten today?"

"Yes, Talia." Lockie glanced toward the window and the last of the day remaining. "It must be dinnertime."

"Would you like me to bring you something? Jules can pack a basket like she used to when you lived in the apartment."

"It was not as bad as you thought."

Rui, our former trainer, was as hard on the apartment as he had been on the horses. There was a streak of casual cruelty in him, which that even still made my stomach churn.

I needed to get those images out of my head.

"Where did you live when you worked for Gesine in Germany?"

"In the attic."

"No."

"It was not a miserable garret like something out of a Victorian novel. There were windows on two walls, a wood burning stove for heat, a small kitchen and a big bed. One of the German girls, who was a student, was assigned to do the housekeeping for me, just like is done here. I was very comfortable."

"The German girls must have been pretty."

Lockie nodded.

"Blond."

"Not all of them."

"Were you ever homesick?"

"No. When I left America, there was no timetable. I didn't know if I'd be back in two years or ten. That was fine with me."

"Why did you come home?"

"Not home. I don't really feel as though I had a home until now. I had an offer and Gesine pushed me to take it, knowing she was on the verge of leaving the business."

"Do you ever speak to her on the phone, write letters? She seems to have been a friend."

"I call her. She calls me. We talk about old times. I tell her about my new times and she knows all about Herr Geist."

"What does she say about his swish?"

Lockie smiled. "I did tell her about that. Gesine said there are two things we can do. The swish springs from his delight in being here. We can make him less joyful and have an unhappy athlete or we can embrace his quirk and accept the small score deductions when he competes. Life and horses are unpredictable. We're better people if we accept that."

"I think you know my choice."

"Yes. If you still want me to show him this season, I will, but I can't imagine he'll be so joyful to find me riding him instead of you. I'm more likely to get resistance than a swish."

"I'll talk to him about it," I said.

Lockie stood, took my hand, and helped me to my feet. "Let's go have dinner. Then if I'm very lucky, you may consent to come back here with me."

I shrugged. "If there's nothing else to do. Maybe."

My father had returned from one of his trips, my grandparents were there, Greer, Cap and Jules which meant we ate in the dining room. There was so much talk, I couldn't follow the conversations as bowls and platters were passed back and forth, rolls reached for and drinks poured.

This was how it should be.

Why couldn't it stay like this?

But it wouldn't. Even by tomorrow, someone would be absent, or the phone would ring with news supposedly so urgent and our attention would be taken away from what was so transient.

Jules put her hand on my shoulder. "Eat. That's part of it, too."

***

The carriage house was dark and quiet.

"Don't leave again."

"Silly."

"I know you will and I know you will come back, but still, don't go."

Across the expanse of the bed, he reached for my hand.

"I'm not supposed to say things like that, am I?" I said.

"How would I know that I'm wanted if you didn't?"

3

THE WEATHER HAD IMPROVED by the next morning and there was a promise of a warming trend. I hoped it would hold until the parade but even Mark Twain knew better than that.

After the early chores, Lockie turned out McStudly in the ring by himself and we went to the house for breakfast. My father and grandparents hadn't started their day yet but Greer and Joly were just finishing his walk.

"Greer, I'd like you to ride the colt for me this morning," Lockie said as we went into the kitchen.

"Absolutely not."

"You saw that—"

I shook my head at him.

"—he has a nice temperament."

"I didn't see that!" Greer threw her jacket at the peg. "I saw him throwing a fit in the trailer and then dragging two big men through the yard."

"If I ride him first, will you get on him?"

I pulled my gloves off then washed my hands at the kitchen sink.

"Why aren't you asking Talia to ride him? Why do I have to be the guinea pig?"

"You're very good on a strong horse."

"So he's strong? You're admitting he's strong?" Greer poured herself a cup of coffee.

"Yes, he's big, young and full of himself. If you don't want to ride him, Talia will get on him for me."

I stopped in mid-scrub. I didn't want to ride that horse either.

"Let the blond guy ride it, it's his horse."

"It was bought to sell. We need to put some weight on him and some basic training, until then it stays."

Greer was silent for a long moment as she glared him. "This is not the kind of horse we should have at the farm."

"We're going to have a great variety of horses here in the future. We have to buy young horses and put some mileage on them because we can't afford to deal in made rides. That's reality."

Having lost my appetite, I sat and did nothing.

"Will you be available for a training session on Citabria this morning?" Lockie asked as he sat at the table.

34

"No."

"When is a good time for you?"

"When is that blond guy going back to Florida?" Greer replied.

Lockie took a breakfast bun from the basket as Jules brought a platter of scrambled eggs and sausages and placed it near him. "The same day as I am."

Jules sat next to me. "Greer, could we have breakfast without a side of argument?"

She stood up, leaving her food untouched and walked out of the room.

"Sometimes there is no right way to say anything to her," Lockie said as he began to eat his eggs.

"Excuse me," I said.

"I'll keep your plate warm for you," Jules said as I left the room and went upstairs.

I tapped on her door. "Greer. May I come in?"

"Yes."

She was at her desk starting to work and I sat on the edge of the bed.

"Lockie went to Florida for you and is staying to give your horse experience. We know how you feel about Cam but please don't take it out on Lockie."

Greer sat immobile for so long I was going to get up and leave. "Lockie came home to be with you. You spent the night together holding hands?"

"Yes."

"When I...I was propositioned. No one wanted me...I'm just a body. A receptacle."

"Greer. That's not true."

"Let's face reality. It's true and it's my resume. It's going to be my traveling companion for a long time."

"Why should you care about what anyone thinks?"

"Because that's the expectation of me. What happened in Florida will happen again and again."

"Are you suggesting your dalliances were so outside the norm on the show circuit?"

"No, but they don't care and I do now."

I nodded. This was such complicated territory to navigate. "You made a mistake. Don't make it again," I said. "Find new ones to make. I always do."

Greer turned back to her paperwork.

"New people will come into your life."

She didn't reply.

I stood. My mother would have known what to say to her but I was at a loss. "See you, later. Maybe you'll help me with the Zuckerlumpens."

Lockie was already at the barn by the time I made it to breakfast. Jules held me out the basket filled with buns and tea and I left the house.

How would it be possible for Greer to avoid Cam? Her workspace was in the lower barn and that's where the sales horses were living. His horses were at Bittersweet and he had dug in. Unless Cam stopped riding for Teche, found another stable who wanted him, and gave up the idea of ever getting Remington back, he was going to be at the farm constantly.

I doubted there was anything he could say that would help Greer get past the incident. She believed Cam thought of her as good enough for a sexual interlude but not good enough for a relationship. According to Cam, he was trying to comfort her in the way he knew how.

It was miscommunication at the least.

I didn't know that Cam wanted a relationship with Greer so, in a way, she was right. However, there was something sweet, even if a little clumsy, for him to make a gesture toward her when everyone on the showgrounds were talking about nothing else but Greer calling the police on one of the top riders in the country.

How this could be resolved was beyond me.

Lockie was in the indoor on McStudly, doing a clockwise volte. Since horses race counterclockwise in America, they really only know one direction and tend to be stiff in the other. The program would be to get the colt balanced and flexible by introducing some basic dressage, then let him go to someone interested in a long-term project. It would take a couple years to get the colt to the point where he could be legitimately called trained.

For about fifteen minutes, I watched the slow and deliberate work and, as always, was so impressed by Lockie's ability. So elegant, so precise, I never got tired of seeing him ride.

Lockie brought the colt into a walk and turned to the center of the ring. "Will you ride him now?"

I had my helmet with me. It was just about the last thing I wanted to do. "Why?"

He dismounted and held his hands together to give me a leg up. "It's part of your education."

I didn't move.

"What concerns you?"

"That you know how to do both less and more than I do. He'll know that the moment my butt settles into the saddle."

"I don't understand. What does knowing anything have to do with it?"

"You are more in control of your body. You have all those years of training and I have a few months."

"You ride CB."

I almost laughed. "He's like a school horse."

"Is that what you think?"

"Yes."

Lockie shook his head. "He's a very hard horse to ride."

"The swish is nothing."

"The swish is nothing. It's everything else. He's very demanding and opinionated. He wants the rider in the exact right place on his back. He has very little tolerance for people. That's why he was sold in Germany. Everyone had enough of him at the barn. Everywhere he goes, he makes himself unpopular."

My pet pony? "No."

"Yes. When we were in Pennsylvania, you wanted to ride him. I thought you'd make it around a couple times and decide he wasn't for you. Trust me, we were all surprised when you rode him on the buckle and wanted to bring him home."

"Why didn't you tell me?"

He gestured with his hands for me to mount. "Why spoil a perfect romance?"

"Greer got on him and said he was like steering a bumper car."

"And you didn't believe her? Get on."

"What if this guy runs off with me? That's what he's been trained to do."

"Turn him in a small circle if he gets too quick for you."

I put my knee into Lockie's hands and was boosted on McStudly's back. He still had a hold of the reins.

"Just relax. Walk quietly until you feel comfortable."

"Then what?" I asked, gathering the reins as Lockie released them.

"Run around until you wear him out."

"Very funny."

I turned the horse toward the track.

"Are you okay?"

"Yes."

"Excellent. I'll be back in about ten minutes."

"You do not leave this building!"

Lockie laughed. "Talia. You're not relaxed."

Keeping light contact with the colt's mouth, I took a deep breath and tried to think how I would ride CB out in the woods.

"He's fine. Don't expect the worst."

There were so few times in my life that I didn't.

"Are you okay?" I asked.

"What do I have to do with this?"

"Just answer."

"I saw the doctor in Florida. Dr. Jarosz sent my medical records to him so he was familiar with the case. He made some suggestions for how to deal with the headaches. And if you can carry on a conversation about my medical situation while you're riding that horse, you can't be that concerned about being on him."

I thought about it for a moment. "Right."

"Could you ask him for a trot?"

I closed my legs slightly on the colt's sides and he went into a fast trot.

"Use your fingers on the reins. Get a feel of his mouth. Remind him that you're there and he needs to come back to you. Slow your posting. Use your weight. That's right."

We trotted once around the outside.

"Volte. He's not going to bend. Give him room to keep his balance. Yes."

Sitting back, I halted the colt. "I can't do this right now."

"Do you have an appointment you just remembered?"

I turned the colt toward him. "Yes."

"You're training a horse. Would it be impolite if I asked what would be more important?"

I stopped next to him and leaned over. "Kiss me, Lockie."

His lips lightly touched mine and lingered longer than usual, then he moved away. "Silly, you make it almost impossible to leave."

"I'm sorry."

"I know you well enough to know there's some part of you shouting 'yes!'."

The truth was difficult to avoid. "Yes."

"Ride the horse. We'll...take CB and Wing for a hack later."

"The Zuckerlumpens will be here later."

"After that then. Inside leg at the girth. Big circle. Work the bit in his mouth. Yes. Did you feel him soften?"

It was a momentary improvement as he started leaning on the bit again.

"Circle again, a little smaller. He's so downhill, we need to get him to shift to his weight to his hindquarters and find some balance. If anything goes wrong, he'll fall on his nose."

Maintaining contact with the outside rein, I squeezed the inside rein as we circled.

"Better. CB's taught you a lot," Lockie said.

"You did."

"I can't take much credit for it."

"Do I have to come there and kiss you again?"

"I take full credit for it. The Schtumpenyanker did nothing. Please make a serpentine."

"Did Greer tell you that's what she called him?"

"Yes. Don't let the colt get ahead of himself. Don't be afraid to put your leg on him."

"Isn't that the gas pedal as far as he's concerned?"

"He has to get used to having a leg on his side and it doesn't mean gallop."

We got to the track and even though I asked for the colt to turn, he didn't and there was confusion.

"My fault," I said as I avoided running into the wall.

"Conviction, Tal. We'll dial him back later."

It wasn't what anyone would recognize as a serpentine but we made our way across the ring a few times then Lockie had me walk.

"That's enough for one day. You did very nicely on him."

"It didn't—"

"Don't negate what I just said. You rode him well."

He took the bridle and I dismounted as Poppy raced into the ring.

"Stay back," I said.

"Oh, Talia. Just let me pet his nose."

"Go get Tango and pet his nose."

Shaking her head, she turned.

"I'll take him, you do your lesson."

Poppy arrived first on Tango, Gincy on Beau a few minutes later, then Greer.

"Don't worry. The blond guy isn't here," I said. "Are you here to help?"

"Yes."

4

THE WEATHER HAD TURNED and the rain started coming down during dinner. It wasn't cold enough to cause icing problems yet but in the middle of the night when the temperature dropped, the ground was going to get slick. It was good that all the horses were inside.

"This is the best time of day." From my seat on the couch, I watched the flames engulf the logs in the fireplace.

"Better than riding CB?" Lockie asked sitting beside me.

"Best time of day not on horseback."

"Is it better than eating a meal with your family around you?"

I sighed. "It's the best time of day not on horseback and not having a feedbag tied to my head."

"Is it better than waking up next to me?"

"It's the best time not on horseback, not eating and not waking up."

"Is it better than falling asleep together?"

"Lockie."

"So it's really not the best time of day."

"You do this on purpose."

The phone started ringing and he reached for it. "Of course I do. Hello." There was a pause. "Hi. Yeah. Sure." Lockie put his hand on my leg. "Uh huh. Just a minute. Tali, would you get me a piece of paper and a pen?"

In the desk drawer, there was a pen and notepad I had left for him. I handed them over and he wrote me a note. "This is a man who wants to buy a horse. Big $."

I gave him a thumbs up and went to tend the fire. We burned a few small logs in an evening but it wasn't for heat and it was almost more of a chore than it was enjoyable. The fire had to burn out before we went upstairs for the last time.

In the kitchen, I heated water, made chamomile tea and brought it back to the living room on a tray with a few cookies left that Jules had sent over. Lockie was just hanging up the phone.

"That's someone I knew when I got out of Juniors and he saw me ride in Florida a few weeks ago. He asked if Counterpoint is for sale."

Greer had sold the last of her horses when she let Sans Egal go down the road. She'd never part with Counterpoint or Spare or Citabria now. She was going to collect horses for the rest of her life. And of course there was Remington.

"You said no."

"Who could face Greer's wrath and sell one of her horses?" Lockie smiled as he took a sip of tea.

"What are we going to do with them?"

"I'm not particularly worried about it. Counterpoint's very impressive showing so far in Napier brought us at least one customer. We would have had two if you didn't decide you absopositivelutely had to keep Kyff."

"He's for you."

"Yes, you said that but we lost a paying boarder."

"That's less important than giving Kyff a good life here where he'll be understood."

"It's a goal in my life to make sure Kyff is understood."

I finished my tea. "He will make a star of you."

Lockie laughed. "He'll make me look like I learned how to ride at clown college."

"You'll see."

He put his empty mug on the tray. "Kyff is more likely to jump the standards than the fences but I spit in the face of embarrassment. Let's go to sleep, Silly."

***

Lockie mounted Kyff and settled into the saddle. "Okay. You've been training him for me. What do I need to know?"

46

"Lockie," I protested. "I'm riding him until you get home."

"So you haven't done anything?"

"I don't know how to do anything!"

"Oh." He steered the black horse into the arena, walked around once, then picked up a trot.

Kyff was a big horse, one of the most substantial we had at the farm where most of the horses were well over 16 hands. Wingspread was 16.2 and, being a Thoroughbred, he was lighter boned than the warmbloods we acquired routinely.

Lockie pulled the gelding back to a walk. "Would you go tack up CB and we'll go for a hack. Give me about ten minutes with him, okay?"

"Sure."

CB was glad to see me, and while he had gone out yesterday, we didn't go for a ride so the appearance of his saddle made him prick up his ears.

"I want to talk to you," I said. "I've been hearing things about you. Not such good things." I put the pad and the saddle on his back. "Someone, no you don't need to know who, said you were a naughty boy in Germany." I tightened the girth. "Is that true?"

Stepping to his head, I looked at him.

I put my forehead on his. "Why did you choose me? I'll bet you thought I was a pushover and that if you got me on your side, you'd never have to move again. Gotta hand it to you. You were absolutely correct."

In one easy movement, I slipped the halter off and the bridle on.

"I wish I was as smart as you." I led him to the mounting block and got on. "Let's see how Lockie is doing on Kyff."

We entered the indoor and found Lockie cantering Kyff easily around. When he saw us, he pulled up and came over to us.

"You've done a nice job with him."

I looked down at CB's mane. "I just rode him."

"Obviously it worked so keep going."

We both walked into the yard and started down the driveway.

"I don't want you to come back from Florida and have to undo my mistakes," I said.

"That's very nice of you to be concerned but you're doing a good job and you can't ruin any of these horses in three weeks. The end of the month I'll be home. You can hang on that long?"

"No."

"You can. I'll be home during the week. It will feel much different," Lockie assured me.

It didn't really work. "I hope so."

"Would you like me to write down suggestions for what exercises you can do with the horses when I'm away?"

"Yes, that would be helpful."

He smiled. "I aim to please."

"Lockie—"

Jules opened the kitchen door. "Could you come here so I don't have to shout?"

We turned off the driveway and crossed the frozen lawn.

"I just got a call from Gram," she said.

Lockie looked at me.

"Former boyfriend."

"Friend," Jules corrected.

"Co-worker," I added. "He has a restaurant in Westchester."

"They're having a re-opening tonight. It's called *Tendrils* now and since Gram's the head chef, he's invited us."

"All of us?" I asked.

"Yes. Your father, grandparents, Greer, you two, Cap if she'd like to go. But not the blond guy."

Cam had become He Who Cannot Be Named in front of Greer and she wouldn't go if Cam was going. That was a given. I hadn't seen him all day so, fortunately, he wasn't available to invite or avoid inviting.

"When do we have to leave? I have the Zuckerlumpens coming in a while."

Kyff pooped on the lawn.

"Nice work, pal," I said.

"I hope it's not an editorial comment on the restaurant," Jules replied. "Are we going? We need to leave around five."

I looked at Lockie and he nodded.

***

As we entered the restaurant, instead of noticing the décor, I realized how beautiful Greer was. I had known it but never appreciated it before. The Kensington-Rowes may have been wolves but they taught her how to glide through a room and I watched as heads turned to her.

Our table was in a prime location and Gram came out of the kitchen to greet Jules with a kiss on each cheek. Introductions were made and we sat among the fine clientel of the area.

A waiter brought menus and there was a moment of silence.

My grandfather flipped the menu over in confusion. "Where's the dinner?"

"Is this a salad bar?" My grandmother asked.

"Gram's a vegetarian," Jules said.

"We're not," Grandfather Shay replied.

Lockie laughed. "Look at this, Tal." He pointed to the menu. "Grilled tofu steak in the style of a rib eye. How do you do that?"

"What's tofu?" My grandfather asked.

"White vegetable sponge," Greer replied, not looking up from the menu.

"No wonder I avoided it all these years."

Lockie laughed at every entrée. "The only thing missing is the serving of Your Panties Are Showing goat cheese."

"Excuse me. What?" my father asked.

"Ignore him, he'll be like this all evening," I said softly.

Some things he couldn't remember but Lockie would never forget the dinner we had at the goat farm inn where I ate cheese covered in soot. I don't know how I choked it down.

We found something to order and our salads were brought to the table. Jules was the only one who picked up her fork.

"Did they get the order wrong?" My grandmother asked.

"No."

"Why are there flowers in my salad?"

"They're edible," Jules replied.

Lockie lifted a long green curly strand with his fork. "What's this?"

"A pea tendril," Jules said. "It's Gram's signature ingredient."

We all looked at her.

"Do you have to be a botanist to eat here?" Lockie asked as he placed the fork on the salad plate.

"Try it," I said.

"No."

It was the same tone of voice a horse would use if he wasn't going to get in the trailer. If a horse could speak.

"No wonder you quit dating him," Greer said to Jules. "It was leave or starve to death."

"If anyone is hungry when we get home, I'll make you something."

"I want a filet," Grandfather Shay said. "I thought this was a restaurant where they served food."

"It doesn't seem to be, Dad," my father said.

"I'll have one, too."

"Hands," Jules said. "How many am I making?"

We all raised our hands.

"And pommes frites."

"Yes!"

"I'm not going out to eat with you anymore," I said to Lockie. "Something always happens."

He stood and took my hand.

"Are we dancing?"

"There's no music," my grandmother pointed out.

"I'm going to introduce Talia to my friends from Bedford Hills."

We snaked between the tables and chairs until reaching a man and woman who were motioning to us.

"Lockie! It's so good to see you!" The woman stood and hugged him. "I thought you were in Florida."

"I'm going back tomorrow. I wanted to introduce Talia Margolin to you. Talia, this is Joe and Beth Rochetta. When did I meet you?"

"I think you were fifteen. You rode our hunter, White Tie and Tails at Ox Ridge," Beth said.

"That's right. I had come east that spring to get some experience," Lockie said to me.

"You won the hunter championship and the Maclay," Joe said.

"I just sat there. He is a very nice horse."

No one would believe Lockie just sat on any horse but anyone who knew Lockie would believe how generous he could be.

"You're still at the farm in Connecticut?" Joe asked.

"Yes. Bittersweet. It's Talia's family farm. Stop for a visit after this month and you can see the horses. We have a few that might interest you."

"We'll do that."

"Talia's dressage horse has the kind of potential that you wish for and rarely find."

"Are you showing him?" Beth asked me.

"Mostly we just trail ride," I replied.

The Rochettas were momentarily speechless.

"It's true," Lockie said. "Our training schedule before my last competition with Freudigen Geist was only to give him beer every day then ride him at the show."

"Innovative," Beth replied carefully.

"Talia's very good with him so I defer to her judgment."

They looked surprised.

I tried not to look surprised. "I think our grilled tofu has arrived. It was nice to meet you."

Everyone said their goodbyes and we returned to the table where Grandfather Shay was pressing his plank of tofu with his fork.

"I'm not eating this," he said.

Greer ate a bite of hers. "It doesn't taste like anything if that's your worry."

There were flower petals all over my plate and some more pea vines.

"What are these small round green orbs on top of my fake steak?" Lockie asked.

"Basil caviar," Jules replied.

"I thought caviar was fish eggs." I scraped the things off to the side of my plate.

"You make an emulsion of basil leaves and drop that into a chemical solution which causes the liquid to form a round."

I squished one of the things with my fork.

"If this is a vegetarian, organic restaurant," Greer began, "why are they putting herbs into a chemical bath?"

Jules shrugged. "I don't know. It's a fad."

"I don't understand this food," my father said as he studied what was on his plate.

"It said on the menu the point was to save the planet one meal at a time," I said.

"This plate cost fifty dollars. That could feed residents in a homeless shelter," my grandmother said, ever the practical one in any group. "If we clean our plates we'll still be hungry."

"Let's not go there," Greer replied as she ate some of the crunchy peas, then pushed her plate away. "They're raw."

"Eating raw saves energy," Jules said. "It was on the back of the menu. The mission statement."

"I have an idea. Save energy and save food by not eating," I said.

Lockie laughed.

Greer put her napkin on the table. "Is it time to go home? Unless someone is looking forward to the sand pudding with agave and new mown hay dessert?"

Jules smiled. "That's not fair. Gram is a fine pastry chef."

"He just doesn't know how to cook dinner." I put my napkin over the plate to give it a decent burial.

"Let's go," my father said and pushed his chair back.

At that moment, Gram arrived from his tour around the dining room, greeting all the customers. He leaned over and kissed Jules's cheek. "Hi, darling. How was your meal?"

Darling?

Lockie looked at me.

"It was delicious," Jules said. "So creative."

"And so filling," my grandmother added.

"Jules, would you mind giving the Times a hundred word review? It would help get the word out," Gram asked.

"No problem at all, Gram. I'd be glad to help."

Half of us were heading to the door as I grabbed Jules's hand.

"She's our designated driver and we have to get home to walk the puppy," I told Gram practically dragging Jules out of the restaurant.

The non-dinner was much remarked upon during our real dinner. Greer and I helped Jules grill the beef, make the salad, and prepare the potatoes. We had hazelnut cookies for dessert with a choice of hot beverages. Much more than we were offered at *Tendrils*.

"We are so lucky Jules has chosen to stay with us," Lockie said as we got into bed later that evening.

"Chosen?"

"Of course. With her ability, she could get a job at any restaurant."

Even thinking about it made me unsettled. "She said that wasn't for her."

"So that was a choice. We're fortunate she chose to be here instead of home in California."

"Tch."

"Go to sleep."

"He called her darling."

"Has she said anything about dating him? Does she go out?"

"She visits friends and...goes to the city. I never thought about her having a boyfriend. Especially not a strict vegetarian like him. What do they have in common?"

"I'm sure it doesn't mean anything."

"What if she left us?"

"Talia, please."

"Maybe she needs more of a social life. Maybe she misses all the activity of Los Angeles. Newbury is quite different and some would say boring."

"Life at the farm is the opposite of boring," Lockie said.

"You know what I mean."

"Many people live in Newbury and enjoy it. Victoria, fresh from the capitols of the world, seems to manage quite well here."

I sighed. "That's true and I wish it wasn't."

"Today is officially completed. I'm leaving tomorrow. You have a lot to do." Lockie rolled over and kissed me. "Go to sleep and dream about basil orbs."

5

CAM ARRIVED EARLY. He rode Jetzt and McStudly while Lockie rode Kyff and Wing.

Greer was in the house working, she said, on the Valentine's Day Parade of Ponies. There was nothing left to do. Aly Beck, Poppy's mother was going to bring Tango Pirate and Gincy's pony, Beau Peep. The Newbury 4-H Horse Club was going to participate. We had made arrangements with the town hall.

She didn't want to see Cam and that was fine. I didn't understand how she could avoid him forever, but seeing her try had some entertainment value.

Cap and I played ground crew, setting and resetting rails, ground lines and moving standards.

Kyff was in light work, exercise more than training. Anything I asked him to do was fun with no pressure.

Wanting him to get the idea that Lockie was his main rider and not me, we made sure no one rode him two days in a row. Cap would get on him one day, Freddi another, I'd ride another day. He always went for a hack after a brief workout in the arena. One day I popped him over the pony fences at a trot and that was it.

"You're doing a good job with him, Tal," Lockie said as he dismounted and Freddi traded him Kyff for Wing.

After a few minutes, he pulled up. "He's starting to feel like a hunter."

"You said you wanted to turn Wing into a working hunter."

All the weeks while Lockie was in Florida had been spent on encouraging Wing to lengthen his frame. Young and clever, I thought he'd get with the program eventually. If a judge didn't mind some expression in a hunter, Wingspread would be very competitive. Showing was all so subjective anyway.

Lockie paused. "He was my event horse."

I nodded.

"I know he needed a new job but..."

I walked over to them. "Did you think you were going to event again?"

Lockie smiled. "Maybe I did. Maybe if..."

"I understand. It was the last link to your other life."

"That sounds so ungrateful. This is wonderful. This is my home and I have everything. More than everything."

59

"But it's a change you didn't want to make."

"Kiss me, Tal."

Lockie leaned over and I kissed him.

"How do you get anything done, if you're always kissing?" Cam asked as he went past on the colt.

"Superior focus," I replied.

An hour later, Lockie threw his duffel bag in Cam's truck, they kissed me goodbye, waved, and headed to the airport. Even though it was only for a couple days, it was always better having him at the farm.

Going into the house, I found Jules had a cup of tea steeping for me. I washed at the kitchen sink.

"I'd like to talk to you," I said.

"First, I'd like to apologize for the dreadful meal last night. If I had any idea Gram would be serving truly inedible food, I would have gone by myself."

"Is the farm enough for you?"

"Wow. That came out of nowhere." Jules sat at the table next to me.

"He called you darling," I said.

"And you extrapolated what from that?"

"That maybe you'd like a social life. Maybe you'd like a boyfriend."

"I had one of those. It was a relationship that doesn't bear discussing, really."

"You're young and beautiful, you're stuck here."

"Thank you for the compliments but I'm not stuck here. I come and go as I please. I happen to like doing exactly what I am doing. And I love you, Dolcezza." Jules leaned over and kissed my cheek.

"I love you, too. You're...like an older sister."

"And you're like my younger sister. I treasure you."

"Because of that I don't want you to stay on and miss out on some other great life you could be having."

"This is a great life I'm having."

I sipped my tea, feeling I was mishandling this conversation and trying to think of any way that could explain what I wanted to say.

"What would you like me to do differently so that you're convinced I'm not being held an unwilling captive at this incredibly beautiful and historic farm?"

"When you put it like that—"

Jules reached her arms around me. "Everything in your life is meant for you, Talia."

"For you, too?"

"For everyone."

My grandparents entered the kitchen. "Does anyone want to go out for lunch?"

My father followed them into the room. "Didn't we have enough of eating out last night?"

"We didn't eat. Let's go have Chinese," Grandfather Shay said.

"There's an actual Chinese restaurant south of here," Jules said.

"What's the difference between actual and Chinese take-out?" My father asked.

"They don't serve Chicken Chow Mein slathered in cornstarch sauce," Jules replied, then looked at me and winked. "I ate at Mu Dan on one of my rare days off."

"I'm a gambler," my grandfather says. "We can always get pizza on the way home."

"I'll go get Greer," I said.

***

Late in the afternoon, I was finishing my session with the Zuckerlumpens who were beyond excited about the Valentine's Day Parade. They knew exactly what they were going to wear and how to customize the ponies, having picked up far too many suggestions from the Internet.

My phone rang and since I hadn't yet heard from Lockie, I checked it.

"Hi."

"Sorry I didn't call. No, I didn't forget. We landed and were driven to the show grounds, practically thrown on horses and rode."

"I thought your first classes were tomorrow."

"That's what we thought, too. But it worked out well. Tropizienne won the class and Roux came in third. I don't think he's as much of a jumper as Teche would like. I suspect he'll be going down the road soon."

"If he's not a jumper, he's not a hunter."

"He'd make a junior a wonderful ride."

"You're okay?"

"Yes. I'm with the pony riders. Call me later after you've had dinner."

Lockie laughed. "Anything else?"

"Wash behind your ears."

"I'll write that down. Later, Tal."

"Bye."

I turned my attention back to the ponies. "You're going to have a big day tomorrow. I want you to be here by eight. The parade starts at eleven with you or without you. The event should last about an hour. I want you to be on your best behavior."

"Yes, Talia," they both said solemnly.

The minute I turned my back they'd be giggling, I was sure of that.

Freddi was doing chores in the lower barn, and promised to oversee the girls. She'd keep them away from McStudly, and with everything under control, I went to CB's stall. We played I Bet You Can't Grab My Tongue for a while, then I gave him a carrot cookie Jules had made in quantity. I thought these were so delicious she should make them to sell but then Jules reminded me we were already committed to the Oliver popcorn balls. We couldn't take on new food projects. I didn't know why the horse cookies tasted better than anything on the *Tendrils* menu. They were vegetarian, too.

The sky was dark when I reached the house and entered the kitchen. Greer was setting the table in the dining room because we had so many people for the evening meal.

"The parade may be a little bigger than you expect," Greer said as she saw me poking around the stove trying to determine what we were having.

"How many kids are in the 4-H Club?"

"Eight."

"That's only ten all together."

"But there are three more 4-H Clubs joining us."

"What's the total?" I tried not to glare at her. This was something at which she excelled. A little too well.

"Something over twenty."

"Do you know how many over twenty?"

"Ten more."

"Thirty horses parading around the green?"

Greer nodded. "I called the newspaper and they're sending out a reporter to cover it. Human interest."

"Oh, good luck with this." I pictured ponies and horses running wild everywhere.

"Try to think positively for a change, Tal."

"Good suggestion."

***

It could barely have been colder the next morning as Greer, Jules and I headed to town. The forecast was for snow late in the afternoon. All I could do was hope that the weatherman was right for a change and the precipitation held off until we were all home.

Greer's phone didn't stop ringing all morning as she fielded calls from mothers needing directions, riders asking about pompoms, sparklies and a pony cart pulling a large paper mache heart.

Why had this seemed like a good idea to me?

The upside was that Jules was enjoying the preparation for the event and was looking forward to the Parade of Ponies. I understood it wasn't as good as going out on a date with a cute guy, but it was what we had this weekend.

There were already trailers parked at the north side of the green, which was where we had been instructed to park. However, that was when we had five horse trailers scheduled. Two police cars with strobe lights flashing were on the scene with officers who weren't in the spirit of the parade at all.

"I hope I made enough heart cookies," Jules said.

There was a large box on her lap filled with beautiful cookies, decorated with piped frosting. That was yet another thing she could have made to sell but for the demand for Oliver popcorn balls.

We parked. Greer and I jumped out to help catch a pony who had backed out of a trailer so quickly that his girl lost her grip on the lead rope. He was now cantering toward the jail, which was oddly appropriate.

I managed to get in front of him while Greer positioned herself on the street behind him and blocked traffic. He put on the brakes and his shoes skidded a little on the pavement.

This was starting out to be everything I had imagined all night long.

Aly Beck parked her rig in front of the library and soon Poppy and Gincy had their ponies tacked up. Beau was dressed as a sheep, and she was dressed as a shepherdess. I felt so embarrassed for him. Tango was dressed like, what else, a Tango Pirate with tuxedo pants covering his forelegs and a moustache painted on his nose. Poppy was wearing a flowing red dress three sizes too big for her over her ski jacket and her helmet was decorated with pink felt hearts.

Jules hugged me. "This is wonderful!" she said as a riderless horse galloped southbound across the green just missing the Grill Girl's sample table of double fried fries.

"We're never going to live this down," I said.

"Way to think positively, Tal," Greer said as she opened the box of ribbons that had been over-nighted to the farm.

Just before eleven, all the adults converged at the top of the green in an attempt to organize the riders. As the clock on the courthouse struck eleven, the parade began and I held my breath.

Of course there was always the horse who had to be in front and several who were terrified of being left behind. The rest of them walked proudly down the street to the admiring applause of relatives, friends, shoppers and storekeepers. Doing their job, the police stopped traffic for the time it took to circle the green and the mayor pretended to judge the participants. Greer held the box while he handed out the ribbons.

There was poop everywhere and, as they promised, the riders cleaned up after their ponies.

While the dog club did their thing at the south end of the green, Trish and Oliver passed out popcorn balls. Everyone got samples of the fries and Jules's cookies.

Greer was interviewed by the Newbury Beacon-Eagle, the Town Crier from somewhere and by the Danbury News-Times, for their Internet only edition, not print. Many families took photos and videos of the event and assured me they would post them on My Face and viewtube where this event would live forever until the sun supernovaed.

Finding a spot on a bench, I sat and watched as the crowd dispersed and the cops finally could leave.

Jules sat beside me. "These are the things that make my life great."

"These are the things that make my life great, too."

***

After packing some of my things into one of my show bags, I brought it to the carriage house. The camping out phase was over.

It was beginning to snow as I went to the indoor, to act as ground crew for Cap riding Spare. She looked good on him and didn't mind that he sometimes became a little over-enthusiastic. We had been working on curing him of his rushing and he was making progress.

"Would you like to show Spare this season?" I asked as she pulled up after jumped a gymnastic.

"Yes, but isn't he Greer's horse? Shouldn't we ask her if that's acceptable to her?"

"Since she got Citabria, she hasn't focused on Spare."

"What's his real name?" Cap asked.

"His papered name is Lyric Line."

"That's lovely."

I moved the poles on the ground and motioned for her to take the combination again.

Spare understood the exercise by this point, but the first few times it was presented to him, he managed to step on all of the rails set there to keep his pace in check.

"That was nice," I said after they had done the gymnastic again. "When is Mill returning from South America?"

Cap let the reins loose and Spare stretched out his neck. "We talked about it a few days ago. It's still their summer but coming fall, so I imagine in a couple months. April? He'll be here for a while but Teche wants to send a string to Europe so maybe Mill will go with them."

"This must be so difficult for you. Lockie's not even in another hemisphere and I miss him so much."

"I miss Mill but we're going to be together for the rest of our lives, so knowing that somehow makes the separation easier to accept."

"You knew this as soon as you met him?"

Cap laughed. "No! He thought I was a spoiled brat and I thought he was a graceless brute."

"How did you get past that difference of opinion?"

"Mill is smart enough to see beyond how unhappy I was with my new situation and kind enough to be there to help me. I'm not stupid. That's when I knew he was my present and my future."

"That's beautiful."

"You haven't gotten to know him yet." Cap grinned. "He's stubborn, convinced he's right all the time and unfortunately he's usually proven correct. He ignores the details, and I pay strict attention to my details. He's a big picture person and I'm a little myopic. We try to meet in the middle. Mill has an unbelievable worth ethic and is a great polo player because he's fearless and smart."

Cap walked Spare to cool him down.

"Maybe you'd like to go to Europe with Mill."

"I would like to be with him but polo is not my sport. I loved training the horses but I'm not going to be playing on a team. That would mean I'd be spending a significant amount of time not on a horse. We talked about it. If I could go visit him for a week, that would be fantastic."

"I'll bet we could get Teche to help us out. You'll hitch a ride with him."

"Do you think so?" Cap asked.

I nodded. "You'll have to publicize his Chartier spice mixes wherever you go from then on, but yes, I think so."

Cap dismounted. "I'll be scorching the world one mouth at a time nonstop just as if he was my sponsor."

We walked out of the indoor together.

"I wonder why he doesn't have red saddle pads with his flame logo in the corner," Cap said. "He must have thought of it."

Had he, I wondered.

***

We had dinner in the dining room, and Greer had worked her magic again with red carnations and ferns she picked up at the florist in town. She was the go-to girl for information on the Pony Parade and enjoyed doing so. I was grateful that there were no major incidents and the mayor hadn't banned us from ever stepping foot in Newbury Center again.

There were already videos of the event of viewtube so we watched those during dessert. Even though my grandparents had been there, they enjoyed it again, laughing heartily at all the shenanigans. They thought we were very brave to chase the runaway horses.

It was possible to call it brave or just trying to avoid lawsuits.

While everyone was settling into the den, I helped Jules in the kitchen.

"I had an idea," I started. "You're a wonderful artist."

"With frosting and a pastry bag I'm not too bad. What do you want?"

"As a small thank you to Teche, I thought we could get a red saddle pad and you could copy his logo. Then I'll take it to the tailor in town and he can embroider the design onto the pad."

Jules thought for a moment. "Okay. I hope the saddle pad isn't too sticky with all that piped frosting on it for the embroidery machine. I don't think I can draw it on paper."

She was teasing I knew and hugged her. "Thank you."

***

Turning on the lights and the heat when I entered the carriage house, I opened the refrigerator to see what was needed, and made a list. Even though Lockie ate all his meals at the main house, he still needed the basics here. Milk, bread, cheese, some crackers if he wanted a snack. I wrote fruit on the list, and would pick up some apples at the store. Oranges were in season but he probably had his fill of those.

I turned off the lights, went upstairs, had my shower and got into bed. The snow had turned to hail and it pinged against the windows. It was good that the bad weather had held off for all the riders so that they could enjoy the day, even if it had been cold.

The phone rang, I checked it. Ryan Saunders.

"Hi Ryan."

"Hi Talia. Ding is catching the first transport north on Sunday after my last class so he should be there on Monday."

"Okay. When should I expect you?"

"My vacation is the third week of the month but I can get out of school early on Friday. Is there someplace to stay in town? A hotel?"

"Absolutely not. Poppy Beck's mother has a spare room. I talked to her and you are welcome to stay with them."

"No. That wouldn't be right. I'll be fine at a hotel."

A child alone at a hotel was the definition of not fine. I had such a strong inclination to talk to her father on the phone but feared I would say things I'd regret.

"Ryan, you can't ride with me unless you have adult supervision. Don't you have a nanny or a guardian who looks after you?"

"I don't need anyone during the school year. School looks after me." She said it with so much confidence that I almost believed her.

"At Bittersweet Farm you won't be rattling around the countryside on your own. It's the Becks or nothing."

"Okay. I'll pay them, of course."

Twelve year olds should not be thinking of sleepovers as a business transaction.

"I'm sure a gift basket or some flowers would be sufficient."

"I'll have my father's assistant send something. Take care of Ding until I get there."

"Yes, Ryan."

Right. I was going to turn a pony, that cost more than a house, out in the pasture and leave him there until his little mistress showed up.

"Bye, Talia."

"Bye, Ryan." I clicked off the phone.

My phone rang again.

"Hi."

"Hi, Silly. Where are you?"

"In your bed."

"Good."

***

Greer was on Citabria, working over the same gymnastic I had used with Cap.

"I was thinking about Spare." I raised the height of the oxer by one hole. "Cap's been working him and I was wondering if you'd object to her riding in a couple classes at the schooling show next weekend."

"Does she like him?"

"Yes. They're quite compatible."

"I don't even know him," Greer admitted. "I didn't need two horses, now I have three."

"You don't want to sell him, do you?"

"No. That's out of the question."

"Unless you're going to come up with a circus act in which you ride three horses at once, you need to figure something out. Do you want to show him?"

"No, not this month. On top of everything else, we have the get-out-of-high-school-free test."

"When is that again?"

"About ten days. Have you studied at all?"

"As long as I pass, what's the difference?"

"I feel the same way." Greer walked Citabria around me. "Is this us talking?"

"Us or clones from another planet."

"If Cap wants to show Spare this season, all I ask is that she treats him with the same care she shows Bijou."

"I will pass along your concern but I don't have any doubt she will. She's fond of him."

Greer nodded. "What are you going to put her in?"

"There's a low jumper division that will suit him and it's in the morning so we can leave by lunch."

"You do hate horse shows."

"They aren't my favorite activity," I admitted. "Take Citabria over the combination again."

"Do you have any suggestions?"

There was a first time for almost everything and I certainly had never given Greer any advice before. "If you really want one, stay over your feet."

"Are you kidding me? I'm not on his neck, am I?"

"Old habits are hard to break and I'm just reminding you. You have a tendency to anticipate. Let him carry you."

"I'm trying."

"You're doing a good job. Let's shoot some video of you tomorrow and you can judge for yourself."

"I believe you but I would like to see my position." Greer picked up a trot and headed for the first element.

"Wait. Wait. Wait."

They completed the combination perfectly. She was such a beautiful rider. So lady-like.

"Much better. Are you done on him?"

"Yes." Greer dismounted.

"The ponies are going to a show next weekend," I said as we left the indoor.

"Yes, I remember."

"Sideshow Ding and Ryan will be here."

"Do what you think is right."

"We can't take that pony of hers to a schooling show. It's not fair to the other kids riding woolly mammoths."

"What's your solution?"

"Ryan'll feel left out if she doesn't go, so I think she should ride Call."

Greer laughed. "She's probably never ridden a pony like that."

I knew what Greer meant by like that and it was true. Ryan has undoubtedly been riding the best and most expensive ponies from the start of her career. That was fortunate for her but somewhat unrealistic. Most riders, juniors or adults, couldn't afford the finest of rides. Ryan, on her own, couldn't afford that pony. Babysitting for a thousand years wouldn't do it.

It wasn't until Lockie had come to Bittersweet Farm that Greer's sense of equine value had been recalibrated. Now we rode green horses, or in the case of CB, something who was such a pain in everyone's neck that they couldn't wait to send him down the road. Kyff was a major brat and McStudly was right off the track. Citabria was green. Counterpoint had taken focused work to get him into low jumpers. Spare was just ready to start schooling shows.

This was work I had never imagined doing but I loved it. I wasn't training horses so they would win ribbons, I worked with them so they would be better partners whether they were destined to show or to hack. I worked with Gincy and Poppy so that they would be horsewomen in tune with their horses who had thoughts and feelings. The girls had to be better partners, too.

I didn't know what I could do for Ryan. She had everything money could buy and I wasn't sure she was in love with her pony. For me, that was essential. How could she know what affection or compassion was when she wasn't experiencing it herself? It wasn't something I could teach to her. She might learn some behaviors but the feeling wouldn't be there.

I knew what it was like to grow up being a strange little girl but at least I had known love. That was never in doubt.

No matter how much I felt sorry for her, she had bigger problems than being a winning rider.

6

"I'M GOING TO BE LATER THAN EXPECTED," Lockie said.

I juggled the phone so I could hear him more clearly. "Where are you?" I thought he would say Napier.

"New Orleans."

"Why?"

"Teche is my ride and he had business to attend to."

That made sense. "Before dinner?" I asked.

"I don't know. I'm at a café right now. He's in a business meeting."

"Do you feel all right?"

"Yes."

"Do you have anywhere to lie down?"

"No. He didn't take me to his house. I had the choice of going to his office or to the French Quarter. I passed a strip club a few minutes ago. That would be a good way to kill some time."

"Kill time there and I'll kill you when you get home. Just saying," I said.

"Then I'll hardly tell you if I did, will I?"

"If you stink of cheap perfume, I'll know."

"I'll air off by then."

"We'll see if you pass the sniff test."

"Talia, will you be waiting for me?"

"Of course."

"Then I really better find a place to take a shower. I call you when we are ready to go wheels up."

"Okay. Say goodbye."

"Bye, Tal."

"Bye, Lockie."

***

He woke me up when he came into the bedroom.

"Hi. What time is it?"

"Almost two." He pulled back the covers and got into bed."

"What happened?"

"We had dinner at a famous restaurant. Then we flew to Connecticut."

"How do you feel?"

"It's good to have you here. It was a long day."

I could translate that. Lockie was worn out.

There were very few people who knew anything about the after-effects of the accident and we didn't think there was any reason for the world to know. But that created situations like this when Lockie needed to quit and he couldn't easily get away.

"Would you cover for me in the morning?" he asked.

"Sure, that's no problem. Stay in bed as long as you want."

"Thank you," he replied and fell asleep.

***

At 6 a.m., it was dark when I left the carriage house. Lockie was still sleeping and I hoped I wouldn't see him for hours. There was nothing important he had to do at the barn, and a day off would be far less than he deserved.

I wondered if he had taken on too much with the showing and commuting back and forth to Florida. It probably wouldn't have been a problem if they had flown directly from Napier to Connecticut but a side trip to New Orleans which lasted the better part of the day was exhausting. Saying anything wouldn't help. This was his decision and it was only for a few more weeks.

We would try to make his time at home as relaxing as possible. Then I remembered Ryan would be arriving on Friday and staying for about eight days. Wherever she was, complications arose. Luckily, Lockie would be in Florida while I took the girls to the show.

As soon as our morning chores were done, with Greer's blessing, I got Cap up on Spare and began to get ready for the show that next weekend. Even if it was a small schooling show, even if it was in the winter, Bittersweet Farm had always maintained its standards. Spare and the ponies would be perfectly turned out, with manes and tails braided. Boots would be wiped clean at the last moment before entering the ring. Hoofs would be brushed off. This was not for the judges, this was for us.

"Did you bring your show clothes with you," I asked as Cap completed a small course.

"I haven't shown since I lived here. I just have what I ride in."

"That's okay. Go to The Horseberry Tack Shop and get whatever you need. I think I'll send for some saddle pads in our stable colors. Is that a good idea?"

"Excellent!"

Greer entered the ring with Citabria. "Do you have time to work with me for a while? Then we could go for a walk?

81

I don't have a lot of time because Amanda's coming this afternoon."

"Sure. That's fine. Cap, when you get done with Spare, would you get CB tacked for me. Then would you get on Kyff after lunch?"

Cap slid off Spare. "No problem. Do you want me to work on Call? You said he might be going to the show this weekend."

"Yes, start polishing him up now."

"Will do," Cap said and led Spare out of the indoor.

"What would you like to work on today, Greer?"

"Flat work. Where's Lockie?"

"Would you like to wait for him? I don't think he'll be at the barn this morning, though, since he came in well after midnight."

"Why? Did that blond guy have anything to do with it?"

"No," I said. "Teche had to get to a business meeting in New Orleans and then they went out to dinner."

Greer steered Citabria to the track. "Did you remember the video camera?"

"I'm sorry. You want me to run and get it?"

"No, we'll just work on the flat today. Sometimes I think I've pushed him along too quickly."

"What makes you say that?"

"Nothing in particular. It's just that I was always in a rush. There was so much pressure on us to reach the finals before we aged out."

"That's true. Was it a terrible disappointment when you didn't make it?"

"It was a relief."

I nodded. "Maybe it just wasn't meant for us. Maybe when something is that difficult it's a message that you're doing the wrong thing."

Greer looked at me, perplexed. "When something is difficult you redouble your efforts."

"I don't want you to misunderstand me. If you're making progress or if you're enjoying the challenge, go ahead but there are times when you can double, triple or quadruple your efforts and you are still not going to succeed."

"I don't agree."

Greer could be unreasonably stubborn. It was one of her worst and best qualities. "What could you have done differently to get to the National?"

"I'm not talking about that. I mean my charity work."

"Come here, Greer," I said.

She turned Citabria to the center of the ring and I walked toward her.

"Bend down. I can't reach you."

"What?" She leaned over.

I kissed her cheek.

Greer sat up. "Fine. Forget the work, just go get the Schtumpenyanker and we'll go for a walk."

"Don't be embarrassed," I said.

"You should be. You're making a huge mistake."

"What's that?"

"You're starting to like me."

I laughed all the way to the barn.

**

Greer and I had a long ride up the mountain and down the other side, talking more about the feedback from the Valentine's Day Parade than anything else.

It had been good publicity for everyone involved. The Grill Girl had called and said there was a line for both lunch and dinner, and take-outs orders had increased. She had been at that location for almost five years and had never seen that kind of business before.

Greer had gotten a call from the Newbury Fair Show Committee with a request to sponsor a class in August. She said yes and asked them if it would be possible to organize a show earlier in the season. They told her to write a proposal with all the details and figures, then they would consider it.

I began to see how Greer's days were so busy there wasn't enough time to get everything done and why she was perfectly happy having just the one horse to ride. This was so out of character for her but maybe it was her character finally coming out.

The wind had picked up and my hands and face were cold after we came back to the barn from our ride, did our noon chores, and went up to the house.

"Perfect. You're just in time to help me make egg noodles," Jules said.

Greer opened the door. "It's time for Joly's walk." He followed her amiably outside and they were gone.

"It's not a three person job, though, is it?" I asked, washing my hands at the sink.

"It's something I do alone at least once a week," Jules replied as she removed a disk of dough from the refrigerator. "They're for the chicken soup you asked me to make."

I glanced to the stove and saw the large stockpot simmering over a low flame. "Did Lockie have breakfast?"

"I haven't seen him yet."

I leaned against the work counter. "I don't know what to do."

Jules dusted the dough with flour. "What are your choices?"

"He came home very late last night and I don't think he feels well. I can be my usual annoying self or I can let him be a big boy."

She cut the dough into quarters. "First off, you're not annoying. You care. We all appreciate that."

"But I get carried away. Not every situation is a crisis."

"I'm going to put the dough in the top of the pasta machine and you're going to crank the handle." Jules showed me how to crank.

I had seen this procedure on television. "They do this on Gourmet TV with an electric machine."

"This is how my grandmother does it."

"Gotcha. Can't argue with grandma."

"What's your instinct on Lockie?"

"I should not trust my instincts. I become a nudge." I cranked the handle of the pasta machine, the dough was rolled flat and came out the other side.

The door opened and Lockie entered the kitchen. "I was looking for you."

"Greer and I went for a hack. I was letting you sleep."

"There's some chicken soup for lunch," Jules said to him as she laid the sheets of dough out on the counter. "Would you like anything else, or would you just like to start with that?"

He sat at the table. "The soup."

"Do you feel alright?" I asked.

"Is it okay if I take a couple days off?"

"Of course. We're fine. There's plenty of help at the barn."

"Do you want to take a vacation? Go somewhere?"

"I want to stay home," he replied.

"I have an idea." Jules began cutting the pasta into strips. "I'll pack you the picnic basket this evening and you don't have to leave the carriage house for dinner. We can do the same thing tomorrow."

Lockie nodded.

Greer came in with Joly. She glanced at Lockie. "You look terrible."

"Thank you for your input, Greer." He stood. "May I have the soup to-go?"

***

At mid-afternoon, when I had a few minutes, I drove to the carriage house to look in on him. "Lockie?" I opened the door.

"I'm awake," he said from the couch.

He looked worse than last time I saw him.

"Did you have lunch?"

"Yes, but it didn't stay down."

I put my hand on his forehead. It felt warmer than it should be to me. "Would you like some tea? I brought some food a few days ago. There are some crackers, peanut butter, some cheese. Cheddar not soot cheese. You should probably hold off on those for a while but please stay hydrated."

He smiled.

"You might have picked up a bug in New Orleans. Cities are teeming with germs."

Victoria had gotten a wool throw in a hunter green tartan pattern as a prop for the photo sessions more than utility. I retrieved it from the cabinet and placed it on the arm of the couch.

Lockie patted the cushion next to him and I sat.

"Are you sure you have enough help? What about the colt? What do you call him?"

"McStudly," I said. "We leave him out for a few hours and he's pretty reasonable. He's eating like a horse, though."

"Are you giving him beet pulp?"

"Yes, and all the hay he wants."

"We don't want to put too much grain in him."

No, we did not. "If you need anything, call."

"Maybe you shouldn't stay here tonight. I don't want you to catch whatever I have."

"That's fine. I'll bring dinner to you, leave it on the front step, knock three times and run away before the germs leak out under the door."

"Wear a Hazmat suit and you can come in."

"I'm not wearing gas mask now so I probably already have come in contact with your bugs."

"I'm sorry. We can't really afford for both of us to be out of commission at the same time."

"I'll be fine," I replied. "You take some time off and do whatever you do when you have your freedom."

"I've never had any so I don't know what I'd do."

"Do you read?"

"Not so much."

"Do you play cards?"

"Yes."

"Would you like to play with my father and grandfather?"

"Who will be the fourth?"

"Greer. She's a card shark."

"Are you serious?"

"One time Victoria left her at a casino hotel in the south of France and went off on a junket. The only way Greer could afford a room was to win at vingt-et-un. None of the men thought this young girl was serious and with that huge mound of chips in front of her, she was seen an easy mark."

"Mistake."

"Big time. She's very self-reliant."

***

Liking to keep the horses perfectly groomed at all times, I was giving CB's mane a quick trim when the horse transport arrived with Sideshow Ding.

"The pony's here," Cap said as she came down the aisle.

Stepping off the bucket, I went to kiss CB on the nose. "He's not cuter than you, just smaller."

"What does this thing look like?" She asked as we went into the yard.

"Breathtaking," I replied.

"Hi," one of the assistants called to us. "He ate and drank. We got him out for pee breaks every few hours. He was no trouble."

Of course not.

Freddi came out of the indoor with Whiskey. "Let's have the unveiling. It can't be as bad as McStudly."

The ramp was lowered and the assistant went into the trailer. A moment later Ding appeared.

"Holy Moly," Cap said as the flaxen chestnut pony walked carefully down the ramp. "I've never seen anything like this in real life and I thought the horses at Country Day School were expensive."

The assistant handed me the lead rope. "Have fun. All expenses were paid so we're set."

Of course.

"Let's hand walk him for a while. If he's okay, turn him out in the ring for an hour or so. We'll take his temperature

90

before feeding. Everyone keep a close eye on him. If he doesn't seem right, we'll get the vet here to check him over."

I was certain Ding was fully insured but that wasn't the point. Nothing should happen to him on my watch.

Greer walked by with Joly close to her. "Is that the movie star's daughter's pony?"

"Sideshow Ding in person. Signed autographs available for a small fee," I replied heading back to CB. "Do you want to play some cards tonight?"

"Why?"

"Lockie is taking a mini-break and he can't go to the movies because it's too loud, he can't read because it gives him a headache, he can't drive at night because of the headlights so I'm trying to find something for him to do. He's exhausted."

Greer shrugged. "Okay, but I'm not going to let him win."

"I wouldn't expect it," I replied.

7

ABOUT AN HOUR LATER, the Zuckerlumpens arrived
and proceeded to lose touch with reality over Sideshow
Ding. At least he took their minds off McStudly.

"My mother said Ryan Saunders is Adam Saunders's
daughter. Is this true?" Poppy asked.

"Yes," I replied as they danced around me.

"The Adam Saunders who was in *Zero Time*?" Gincy
asked.

I had no idea what movies he had appeared in and didn't
care. "Did you see him in that movie?"

"YES!"

"Then it was him."

"She's going to stay at my house! Maybe he'll visit her.
Maybe he'll have dinner with us!"

"I think Mr. Saunders is in New Zealand. Did you tack your ponies up yet?" I replied.

"No."

"You have a show next weekend so if you don't think you need to get ready for it, let me know because I have lots of horses to ride."

As the girls ran off toward the lower barn, my phone rang.

"Hi."

"Did Ryan's pony arrive?"

"Yes, about an hour ago."

"I was asleep so I didn't hear the trailer pass the house," Lockie said.

"I'm glad you could rest. Ding's fine turned out in the ring. Freddi will bring him in soon and check him over."

"He might need another blanket since he's been in Florida for two months," Lockie said.

"I'll see what he's wearing and can swap blankets with Call if necessary," I replied. "How do you feel?"

"Better."

"I'll call after I finish with the Zuckerlumpens and you can tell me if you want to have dinner and a card tournament at the main house."

"Thanks, Tal."

"You're welcome."

***

We had Jules's delicious chicken soup with noodles for dinner. The broth and noodles were one course and then the chicken and vegetables were the next. Lockie had the soup and a little of the chicken and some carrots while the rest of us ate without reservation.

I didn't think he had gotten ill during the trip, but rather that it was just exhaustion and having his routine scrambled. It was still a very good idea for Lockie to take some time off but I doubted that he would be able to sit at home and do nothing for a second day. It wasn't in his experience or his character.

Even though everyone knew he was feeling a bit under the weather, my grandparents grilled him mercilessly on Florida and what it was like to compete on an international show circuit.

"This is normal for him," Greer said. "Lockie's been at this level since he was fifteen."

My grandfather expressed amazement that such a young person could compete successfully against adults. He paused for a long moment. "Then you're not going to get a real job?"

We all laughed.

After a dessert of sponge cake and custard, which Jules thought would not upset Lockie's stomach, we cleared the table, and the card playing began. Jules and I went into the den to watch another of the concocted cooking game shows where the challenge always seemed to feature bizarre ingredients and how the contestants were supposed to turn them into dinner. Usually we fisked the shows as they were in progress, laughing as we did.

"Lockie fits into the family so well," Jules said during a commercial break.

"Yes, he does."

"Why?"

"I'm sorry. What do you mean?"

"Has he ever spoken of his family in California?"

"Not beyond the fact that his father wasn't keen on him taking up riding when he was eight. He hasn't mentioned them since he told me about that last summer. He says this is his home."

"We're perfectly happy to adopt him, aren't we?" Jules asked.

Someone on the television was trying to crush those red hot candies with a rolling pin and turn them into a tart shell. Good luck with that, buddy.

"Change of place, change of fortune," I said. "If California wasn't good for him, Bittersweet can be." Picturing Greer in the kitchen playing poker and beating the pants off all the men, I smiled. If this was an improvement over California, his family life there really had to be worth forgetting.

The show came back on and the audience discovered that the candies melted forming a hard crust requiring a hammer and chisel to break through. I couldn't tell if that was worse than the tart that went into the oven so late that it was uncooked. "Just scrape off the filling and eat it," the contestant suggested.

"If you haven't noticed, sweetie, it's raw," I said to the television.

"Gram called," Jules said as the judges pushed the dessert aside.

"He offered the dessert we tried so hard to avoid?"

"Close. He asked me to be his sous chef on the Great Gourmand competition."

My head snapped around so fast, I was surprised I didn't leave an ear lying on the couch. "Are you considering it?"

"Yes," Jules replied.

"Why?"

Jules didn't say anything for a moment.

"So I was right and being here at the farm isn't enough for you."

"Why did you go to that horse show last month?"

"Sneaky," I said.

"Because it was something different to do. It was to challenge yourself."

"You want to cook on television as a challenge to yourself?"

"You're trying to get me to admit that being here isn't enough for me and that's not true. It's not about any affection I may or may not have for Gram. It's just something else to do."

"We're tedious and boring."

"You went to Florida."

"You're not supposed to come up with a good argument," I said.

"You can come with me. They have an audience gallery, with friends and families of the chefs, cheering them on. Consider yourself a chaperone."

"Does it sound like I'm trying to pick a boyfriend for you or in this case, encourage you to not pick this strict vegetarian?"

"It's just about the food."

"What happens if the grocery item of the day isn't broccoli but beef? Then what does Gram do?"

"Why else would he have called me? He'll wear latex gloves and make me taste test everything."

"You're kidding, right?"

"Right."

"I'll go," I said, "because I don't want you to be alone with him!"

"In a studio full of people?" Jules asked in surprise.

"Stop making sense."

"I'm not interested in Gram now or in the future. But I would still like you to come to the city with me and be there for the taping."

"I'm in."

Greer came into the den and sat next to us. "They're all in, too. I beat the pants off them. Not literally."

"I don't want to see that," I said.

Jules shrugged. "It might be interesting."

"Am I invited, too, or just the good daughter?" Greer asked.

I leaned over to look at her. "The wicked daughter can come too."

Jules explained what the trip to the city would entail.

"As long as we don't have to eat any of his inedible swill," Greer replied.

"I promise to take you someplace nice. Jing Two for Chinese. How does that sound?"

"Good."

Lockie entered. "The card shark took all my money so I'm going home."

"This is your home," Greer reminded him. "What did I win? A dollar-fifty? I'm surrounded by big spenders. In France, I won thousands of Euros and none of the men complained."

"They undoubtedly considered it the price to be in the presence of your comeliness and good company," Jules replied.

"Don't forget my excellent disposition," Greer added.

"The main attraction," I said.

"I'm not complaining," Lockie said. "I just won't play with you again. Have a good night."

"You, too."

"Tal?" He asked.

I stood and followed him to the kitchen.

"I'd like to ride tomorrow." Lockie pulled on his jacket.

"Wing?"

"I'd like to get on Kyff."

"Sure. I'll have Cap get him ready for you."

We stood there in silence for a moment.

"Do you want me to stay with you tonight?" I asked.

"Do you want to stay with me?"

"I haven't experienced a time when I didn't want to be with you," I began.

"Yes, you have. When you called me an idiot."

"Lockie! You were the new Rui as far as I was concerned."

"When did you decide I wasn't?"

"Do I need to know to the minute?"

He handed me my blanket coat. "Put your jacket on and let's go home. We can figure it out there."

***

I was in the center of the arena praying that Kyff would behave. He was generally pretty decent but it was impossible to predict when he would have one of his interludes. There could be bucks or flying sit spins or just refusing to cooperate. Although these moments were becoming more rare, they continued to happen. Still, I thought he was good-natured underneath it all.

Lockie trotted him on the track, keeping light contact with Kyff's mouth, bending into the corners, looking every inch the working hunter. Coming back into a sitting trot, Lockie asked for a canter departure and got an explosion.

Kyff nearly stood on his front legs he bucked so hard and Lockie pushed him forward. There were a few leaps and a lurch as he invented gaits instead of simply cantering.

"Wow," Greer said, coming up to me.

"This is really disappointing," I said, watching Kyff throw one of his temper tantrums. "I thought he was getting past this."

"It'll take longer than a couple weeks," Greer replied. "He may never be trustworthy."

Lockie got Kyff settled back into a trot and got him moving forward with his hind end engaged to minimize the possibility of another series of bucks.

"Who's going to be able to ride him?" Greer asked. "He has to go to a professional."

"I don't want to sell him. Who will have patience for this? Life will be very hard for him."

"We don't even know what his talents are. Is he worth this?" Greer asked, sensibly.

"Someone did this to him," I replied.

"You don't know that. He may have neurologic issues. He may be wired wrong and no amount of training will stick."

"Do vets do equine brain scans?"

"Are you saying we should truck him to Tufts or New Bolton and have a CAT scan done?" Greer asked.

I thought about it for a moment.

"What happens if he has a tumor or something? Are you going to euthanize him?"

"We have to do what's right for the horses, whatever it is," I replied. "We don't want him to hurt himself or anyone else."

Greer watched as Lockie rode around on the now calm Kyff. "Hey, Lockie, do you think this horse is mental?"

Lockie reined back to a walk. "What?"

"Do you think he's brain damaged?"

"Because he plays around a little?"

"That's a little?" I asked.

"Yes. Are you girls talking yourselves into something?"

"Um..."

"I've seen neurologic horses. This isn't one of them. Go get Wing ready for me and stop watching medical shows on television when I'm not here."

"Lockie..."

"Was this a rerun of *House* where someone had a brain tumor and behaved abnormally?"

I looked at Greer and she looked at me.

"Yes, that was the last episode I saw."

"Stick with the cooking shows."

Lockie turned Kyff in the opposite direction and began trotting.

Greer and I left the ring and went to get Wingspread ready for his ride.

I gave CB a piece of carrot as I went past.

"I had an idea," Greer said, following me.

"What's that?"

"You hate horse shows."

"There may be another word for it but that one will do."

"Have you made a plan for what you're going to do this season?"

I opened Wingspread's door. "Why do I need a plan?"

"For the ponies."

"They won't be here." I led Wing to the cross ties and attached the clips.

Greer stared at me. "Where do you think they're going?"

"To someone else." I hadn't actually thought about it very much.

"They're not going anywhere, you're stuck with them."

"I can't...no."

"You didn't think this through, did you, Tal?"

We went to the tack room.

"I told them to find someone else. Just like we're going to find another coach for the movie star's daughter."

Greer shook her head in amazement. "This is the one instance where you've taken positive thinking to a destructive extreme."

"I don't know how you can say that."

"Besides Robert Easton, who is a coach here?"

Robert Easton had being demeaning down to a science. But for those riders who didn't take it personally, he was guaranteed to produce winners. I wasn't always sure he was doing it on the up-and-up but I had learned that wasn't essential to the process. Winning was the goal. The ends do justify the means for some people and he was one of them.

But I was hardly a solution or a replacement for Robert Easton. There were hundreds of kid coaches on the East Coast. There were many excellent trainers with far more experience than I had.

"Families drive a hundred miles to bring their children to a trainer. They live in the city and drive to New Jersey. I'm sorry for their inconvenience but I'm not the droid they're looking for."

"They love you. You love their ponies and you respect them. Because of that, they're never leaving."

"Greer, please, this can't be happening. I have so much to do."

Even with Lockie home at the end of the month, I had a barn full of horses to deal with every day. The number was sure to increase once Lockie and Cam were back from Florida. Then they'd be showing and my time wouldn't be my own.

"There may be a solution," Greer suggested. "I'll take them to the shows on the weekends and you work with them during the week."

I lifted Wing's bridle from the rack. "What about the Ambassador of Good Cheer? There will be weekend events."

"I'm very good at scheduling," Greer replied.

That was true. If Greer wanted to work as an air traffic controller, she could do that and her nails at the same time with no difficulty.

"Think about it," Greer said as she went to Citabria's stall.

"I don't have to. Yes."

***

Lockie finished his morning rides and we walked up to the house together for lunch. The weather was a bit warmer, which only meant that it would rain and not snow.

"I couldn't have a better friend than you," he said.

104

"Are you preparing me for bad news?"

"Talia, please. I'm trying to say something important. You need to stop worrying. If there was something wrong with Kyff, I would tell you. You're doing a good job with him and I'm so pleased I've had nothing to do with it. It's all you."

"I've done such a wonderful job he nearly turned himself inside out with you this morning."

"I've been on horses who have flung themselves to the ground in order to avoid cooperating. Kyff is a cupcake compared to a really bad horse."

"Are you saying I've lead a sheltered life?"

"Yes." Lockie laughed. "You were two girls riding equitation. I don't expect that you would have experienced the same kind of things I have as a professional. I only ask, for your own comfort, that you don't watch medical shows so that the most dire and dramatic illnesses are brought to your attention, and that you don't keep wondering if I want you to stay with me."

"What?"

"I come home to be with you. Is that clear?"

"Yes."

He opened the door.

"Happy Valentine's Day," Jules said. "We have a lunch celebration and a dinner celebration. By tomorrow we will be sick of pink and red hearts."

We cleaned up, and everyone gathered at the table for soup with heart shaped pasta and heart shaped sandwiches.

"Where are the cupcakes?" Greer asked after we had eaten everything.

"No cupcakes." Jules went into the pantry.

"You're famous for your cupcakes," Greer protested.

Jules usually filled them with something surprising and delectable.

She returned with a very plain cake frosted with unadorned white buttercream and we looked at each other. This was unusually tame for her.

"It looks delicious," my grandmother said supportively.

"The dinner dessert will probably be the real fireworks," my grandfather said.

"I'm glad to have cake that didn't come from the supermarket," Lockie replied.

"How do you know this didn't come from The Grocery on the Green?"

"If it did, I'm sure it's good," my father said.

"And easily better than anything Gram could come up with, all gluten/butter/egg/cream-free," Greer commented.

Jules picked up a long knife. "Who is going to do the honors?"

No one said anything.

"Andrew." Jules handed my father the knife.

He stood, lined up the knife, made the cut, and removed the first large section. The look on his face assured me that something was very different about this cake.

"What's with the cake?" Greer asked.

He turned it so we could see inside. There was a three dimensional red cake heart in the middle of the yellow cake.

Cheering, we all applauded so loudly that Joly ran into the next room.

***

With me on CB and Lockie on Wing, we rode up the mountain past the stream, past the fields the farm still had.

"At one time," I said as we came to a halt, "there were no trees here. Just fields."

"How long ago?"

"When my great-grandfather bought the property from the Tapscotts, it was a working farm but shrinking. Abiel was too old to do that much work and World War I changed everything."

"So your great-grandfather must have gotten the farm for a song even in those days."

"Yes. The business, at that time, was in Waterbury and there were closer properties but he fell in love with this farm so the story goes. The Tapscotts had been here before the

Revolutionary War and while no fighting was done here, iron ore was mined in the area and turned into cannonballs. The farm and farmhouse was iconically American. Patriots had sat where we sat this afternoon and plotted against the British."

"I'm sure the house looks very different inside than it did then," Lockie said.

"There is a ledger in my father's desk, where my great-grandfather noted all the work done on the house in his day. You could ask my grandfather what he did with it. I suspect it was more maintenance and some modernizing but mostly landscaping. The pond was a wet spot, so I've been told."

Lockie turned Wing around. "We didn't have any wet spots where I grew up. Everything was dry. The grass is green in the winter, if you're lucky, and then by May it turns into California Gold. Dry. If you're lucky, it starts to rain again in November. It was such a shock the first time coming east in the summer and seeing green fields. I think that's when I knew I wasn't going to stay in California."

"It's beautiful, though," I said.

"Parts of it are like paradise. This is my home now."

We rode in silence down the hill.

"I have to go to Florida tomorrow morning," Lockie said.

"I thought afternoon."

"My ride leaves at nine. I got a call from the pilot before we tacked up."

"Where's Teche?"

"He's back in New Orleans."

"You're the only passenger on the jet?"

"I think so."

"You must be very valuable to him."

"Very!" Lockie smiled.

"I'm serious."

"It's not that unusual for riders to be flown around the countryside by owners."

"Is that true?"

"That's true."

"But just for the best," I said.

"Value is in the eye of the beholder. You think CB is priceless and his former owners couldn't wait to get him out of the barn, out of the country and out of Europe."

"Why are you saying that in front of him!" I reached forward to put my hands over his ears.

"I didn't say it in German. His English is still pretty weak."

I patted CB's neck. "You are priceless to me."

"Every horse is a good horse in the right place," Lockie said.

"Do you believe that?"

"Yes."

"Is this the right place for Kyff?"

"It sure is."

After this morning, I wasn't sure at all. Kyff never bucked like that for me but he wasn't intended to be my ride. He was supposed to be Lockie's hunter. Kyff was farther along in training than Wingspread, and my plan was for Lockie to show him this season as a working hunter. This rodeo style bucking was worse than he had done in Florida and was absolutely unwanted in the hunter ring. I had seen jumpers do it and it didn't matter in that division.

The question I hadn't yet answered was whether Kyff was a hunter or a jumper. He came to us as a hunter but maybe he was misplaced. Lockie didn't have any trouble ignoring the bucks and the horse had to do something with the rest of his career. I couldn't put the Zuckerlumpens on him. They wouldn't be able to stay on through the rodeo routines.

Kyff might have bucked with me at home but there was no guarantee he wouldn't revert to the bad behaviors we had seen in Florida. Nicole Boisvert was an excellent rider and he left her in the dirt. I couldn't expect better results.

"I don't know," I replied as we approached the barn.

"You believed in him in Florida. Give him a chance."

"I don't want him to hurt anyone." I pulled CB to a halt and dismounted.

"While he's been here, has he bucked with anyone but me?"

"No."

"Let's take the time to figure him out. Horses are like puzzles. You don't always get lucky the way you did with the Schtumpenyanker. He fell in love with you. He will protect you."

"You're exaggerating. Horses aren't that much like dogs. He may prefer me for some reason but that's about it. I'm being realistic."

"No, you're reading it wrong. He has a real thing for you. Not that I blame him," Lockie said following me into the barn.

"You prefer me to Greer. That's the bottom line," I said clipping CB to the cross ties by his stall.

"I do prefer you to Greer, and Cam prefers Greer to you. Although he also finds you a lot easier to deal with."

"Wait." I slid CB's bridle off and replaced it with his halter. "Are you saying Cam likes Greer?"

Lockie took his saddle into the tack room then returned. "You know that."

"I don't know if he likes her or if he LIKES her."

"How he wants to define his feelings for your sister is up to him. As with so many things in her life, Greer makes things more difficult than they need be."

"He hurt her feelings," I said.

"That's the way it is in relationships. You run the risk of getting your feelings hurt."

We looked at each other for a long moment.

"I will try not to hurt your feelings," Lockie said. "But I probably will."

"I forgive you."

"You don't know what I've done yet," Lockie replied.

I shook my head. "It doesn't matter."

***

Dinner was a wonderful celebratory affair with all our favorite foods, Greer's fanciful table decorations and good company. We all missed someone or something with all our hearts.

Cap missed Mill who was still in Argentina.

Jules missed her family in California, even though she insisted we were also her family.

Greer, I thought, felt she had missed the opportunity with Cam. He wasn't out of her life but he wasn't the same person to her any longer.

My father and I missed my mother. That would never change.

As for Lockie, I couldn't pinpoint it. Sometimes I thought there was a shadow of sadness that crossed over him that wasn't explained by the accident. Then he would smile and I was certain I was mistaken. I did tend to read too much into everything.

We went home, undecorated for the holiday as it might be and Lockie took a small box out of the desk drawer and handed it to me.

"Happy Valentine's Day, Silly."

I removed the ribbon and lifted the lid.

Inside was a antique Japanese carved horse, grazing, with a smiling rider lying on its neck.

"That's how I think of you and CB. You derive so much pleasure from each other."

I was trying not to cry.

"Sometimes I think you feel that way about me a little."

In the morning, we checked on the horses together, then right after breakfast, a car came to take him to the airport. We kissed and he was gone.

8

EVEN THOUGH I knew he would be back on Monday, this time I found it harder to deal with the separation.

"Stop thinking about it," Cap said as she placed her saddle on Spare's back. "What if I thought about Mill every minute of the day?"

"You'd be sad?"

"I'd be happier than I am."

"Why?"

"He has this terrific opportunity to work with the kind of polo ponies he could only dream of six months ago. We were really struggling to make ends meet at out barn. Mill didn't want to take any handouts from his father. It was enough Soule was helping pay the college tuition." She reached under Spare's belly and grabbed the girth.

"Don't you miss him?"

"Of course, I do. We saw each other every day since the day we met until now. I think about him and I'm happy." She pointed to her face. "See me smile?"

I nodded.

"Think about why this bothers you so much and know it's not the same situation."

I opened my mouth to protest.

"My father was a bigamist. He left us and had another family. What's worse is that I think he loved them better than he ever loved us."

"What a skel."

"I agree. What a dunce. I'm great. My mother's great. His other wife is a bottle blonde with dark roots and they both wear flip-flops everywhere."

"Tch."

"I don't think about my father. Well rid of him."

"It's hard for me to disagree," I replied.

"Exactly. I could be mucking the stalls and thinking Mill's in Argentina. They have those beautiful dark haired dancers down there with the clicker things."

"Castanets."

"Right! What if Mill goes to the local taverna and there's some senorita clicking away at him and like my father, he goes off with her. He finds it hard the first time but it grows progressively easier to forget me. In a few weeks, like my father, Mill's calling me babe on the phone because he can't remember my name."

I laughed. "You have a more vivid imagination than mine!"

"You can't let your history dictate your life."

I stepped closer to her and gave Cap a hug. "Thanks."

"You're welcome."

"I might need the lecture again. I'm a slow learner."

"I'm not going anywhere and neither is Lockie. Spot me on Spare. We have a show this weekend."

***

It was mid-afternoon and the Zuckerlumpens were already tacking their ponies up for a quick session when Ryan arrived in a town car. She got out and the driver opened the trunk to remove several suitcases.

Aly and I went into the yard.

"Hi, Talia."

"Hi, Ryan. This is Mrs. Beck where you will be staying for the next week."

They shook hands.

"Thank you very much for your hospitality," Ryan said.

"Do you need anything from your suitcases?" Aly asked.

"I have everything for my ride today in my duffel bag."

"I'll put the suitcases in the car so we don't forget them." Aly picked them up and left.

"Where's my pony?"

"In the lower barn with the other ponies," I replied and began walking to the other building. "Gincy and Poppy are getting them ready for their ride this afternoon and if you would like, you can join them."

"Okay," Ryan replied with less enthusiasm than I expected.

"We're going to a show tomorrow," I said.

"I can still enter some classes."

"We can do that when we get to the show grounds. You wouldn't be riding Ding, though."

"Why not? Is he lame?"

"He's fine, but we need to be realistic about him. He's at a much more accomplished level than anyone else who will be competing."

"So?"

"It's unfair. The competition didn't just win a pony hunter division on the winter circuit."

"That's not my fault," Ryan replied sharply.

"Why would it make you feel good about yourself to compete against riders who have no chance to win?"

"Winning makes everyone feel good. My father would like me to win."

I stopped. "Here's your choice. You can ride Calling All Comets, a Bittersweet Farm pony, or you can groom for the other riders."

Her mouth dropped open. "I don't groom. People are paid to groom for me."

"Not here. That's not the way this barn runs."

"What was the point in shipping him from Florida?"

I looked at Ryan evenly, believing everything she said was the only way she thought life worked. For someone as privileged as she, that was undoubtedly true. For the rest of the world, no. "To have lessons this coming week so you can learn how to become a more efficient equestrian and to find a coach."

"I've been through everyone."

"Excuse me, what?"

"Everyone around here."

"What do you mean everyone?"

"I've been riding most of my life and my father has very high standards of performance. That's how he's gotten to where he is in Hollywood."

Where was Greer when I needed her?

"If that's the case," I said, "then you will ride Call to the very best of your abilities and make your father proud of your effort."

"Effort? You don't get judged on effort."

"You do here," I replied as we entered the barn. "Ladies. This is Ryan Saunders. Ryan, this is Gincy Hamblett and Poppy Beck."

"Hi, Ryan," Gincy said.

"Hi," Poppy was grinning. "I saw *Zero Time*. It was so exciting. Your father is such a good actor."

"Thank you," Ryan replied. "He is very good. He has a new movie coming out this summer."

"Awesome! What's it called?" Poppy asked.

"*Graft*."

Poppy and Gincy looked at each other in confusion.

"It means a payoff," I told them. "An example would be when a politician is paid off to do as someone wishes, rather than what the citizens want."

They were bored by the explanation.

"Are you ready to ride?" I asked to change the subject.

"Yes!"

"Mount up and I'll be with you after I get Ryan organized."

Poppy and Gincy led their ponies from the barn.

"You can ride Ding this afternoon but you still won't be riding him at the show tomorrow. If you'd like to go to the show, I suggest you ride Call." I pointed to him.

"An Appaloosa?" Ryan asked in disbelief.

"It's not beneath you. He's a terrific pony."

She didn't reply.

"Think about it. Make up your mind. Cap will be around to help you tack whichever pony you choose." I turned and left the barn.

There was nothing that could make me want this child to be at the farm permanently. She had the capacity to be polite but she was spoiled to a degree I would have thought impossible. I didn't blame her, I blamed her father. Obviously, Adam Saunders couldn't make time in his busy career to raise his own daughter. If that was the Hollywood way, that was fine. It wasn't the Swope-Margolin way.

Again, I was left feeling that it wasn't my responsibility to sort out all the life issues Ryan had. I had to double down on finding her a trainer but it was not good news to hear that she had already been with everyone.

What did that mean? Did she kick them free because she didn't win? Did they kick her free because her father was so heavy-handed?

That was probably a good quality to possess if one wanted to be a major action-adventure star.

It was counterproductive for a father.

I went down the aisle to the office where Greer and Amanda were working.

They looked up from their paperwork.

"Ryan Saunders arrived," I said. "She needs to be recalibrated."

Greer put down her pen. "How so?"

"She lives in a fantasy world."

"Are you asking for help?"

"Yes."

"I'll be a half hour, Amanda, is that okay?" Greer stood.

"Maybe Jules has something for tea."

As I headed to the indoor with Greer, I wished I could take a break for tea and the miniature fruit tartlets I had seen Jules making earlier.

After changing into jodphurs and boots, Cap was getting Ryan on Call as we entered.

"Greer!"

"Yay!" Gincy said.

I looked at Greer. "Aren't you popular?"

"Of course. They haven't worked with me yet."

Cap got Ryan's stirrup leathers adjusted and she walked Call to the track.

"Ryan, this is my sister, Greer. Greer, this is Ryan Saunders, the owner of Sideshow Ding."

"He's a very nice pony," Greer said.

"I should be riding him," Ryan replied.

I looked at Greer.

"If you're a good rider," Greer said, "it shouldn't matter what horse you're on."

"Chocolate chip ice cream here?" Ryan said.

Poppy pulled Tango up to alongside her. "Apologize to him!"

Greer looked at me. "Potentially quite unlikeable."

"She was nicer in Florida."

"She needed you then."

"She needs us now."

"She doesn't see it that way. Go up to the house. I think they're live-streaming Lockie's class on the Internet. Let me handle this."

An out. I would take it. "Okay. See you girls later."

I went up to the house and was greeted by Joly. I picked him up for kisses and hugs.

"What are you making?" I asked Jules.

"Cupcakes for the cupcakes," she replied. "I know you'll be home by lunchtime so they can have them for dessert and you don't have to worry about the frosting getting all over their clothes."

I nodded and put Joly down. "Greer is teaching my class now."

"Why?"

"Two reasons. Lockie's ride in Florida is going to be streaming live in about ten minutes and Ryan Saunders is a miniature version of the off-spring of any Hollywood movie star." I washed up at the sink, then went to the refrigerator for something to drink. "Everything is done for her. She's like an adult with nice manners and knows how to behave, but when she doesn't get her way, it makes her jump the tracks. She goes from being adorable to being Lindsay Lohan in two shakes."

Jules laughed. "I grew up with the children of movie stars."

"How many did you kill before you graduated from high school?"

"None, but I tried to poison a few. A well-placed peanut can be a lethal weapon." Jules winked.

"Diabolical."

"Thank you."

"I need to spend time this afternoon trying to find someone near her school in New York to take her on. This is too far for her to go."

"You say."

"I do say that because it's the truth."

"What if she went to The Briar School?" Jules asked as she filled the cupcake liners.

"Don't work out how she can stay here!"

"Let me ask you this."

"Uh oh."

Jules smiled and continued to scoop batter. "Is it valuable for the business of Bittersweet Farm to have a zillion dollar pony in training and winning classes as a rider from here?"

"This kid should not be used for what she can do for any barn," I replied.

"That's such a nice sentiment."

"But you think it's wrong."

"She'll be used wherever she goes."

"What a doomed little life she has."

Jules opened the oven door and slid the sheet tray onto the rack. "I wouldn't say that." She closed the door. "She's a jewel in any farm's crown."

I shook my head and pressed the on button for my laptop so we could watch the Orange Coast Classic then opened another window and searched for a directory of all coaches within a hundred miles of Ryan's school. Every minute or so I'd go back and check on Lockie but there were about a dozen horses ahead of him. Then Cam rode Tropizienne and a few horses later, Tabiche.

"Sally Ebison," I said.

The oven timer began chiming and Jules went to remove the cupcakes. "What, Tal?"

"This girl was just aging out when I moved here. I saw her ride and she was very good. Now she has a barn in Semple. That's close to Ryan's school."

I checked back on Lockie. He still had about twenty minutes before he'd ride.

Picking up the phone I keyed in the number, it rang and was then answered.

"Semple Hill Farm."

"Hi. This is Talia Margolin from Bittersweet Farm. Is Sally available?"

"I just saw her walk down the aisle, let me catch her before she gets on the next horse."

Watching the progress of the Orange Coast Classic, I waited a minute.

"Hi. Sally Ebison."

After introducing myself, I said I had seen her riding in shows as a junior in New York and Connecticut and wondered if she'd consider taking on Ryan and the wonder pony.

Sally wanted to see Ryan ride before making that decision because she had a small barn and wasn't looking for new riders. Of course, having Adam Saunders' daughter there made a difference.

I told her where we were and where we would be tomorrow. If she wanted to stop by, that was fine.

She said she'd try and we hung up.

"Okay." I put the phone down. "That's a step in the right direction."

Jules put a slice of Valentine's Day cake, somehow left over, on the table between us and we settled in to watch Lockie.

"Does he want Ryan to go or stay?"

"I don't know. Poppy already gave her hell. Ryan said something uncomplimentary about Call and Poppy insisted she apologize. How are they going to live together for a week?"

"Poppy is a little firecracker," Jules admitted as she cut into the cake with her fork.

I took a bite of cake. "Now that Greer has calmed down—"

"She has?"

"For her. It would be better to have peace for a little while. I don't want Poppy and Gincy to start comparing their ponies to Ding. Ryan will be given everything she

125

wants and more. Neither the Hambletts nor the Becks can afford that. Tango Pirate and Beau Peep are really nice ponies. That should be enough. There's no reason for them to feel they can't compete with Ryan."

"It's a difficult situation," Jules admitted. "On one hand you have unlimited money and on the other you have regular people who can't afford everything."

"This was how I felt with Butch. I love him, don't get me wrong. He was my only friend here. But I knew that he couldn't compete against the horses in the ring with me."

"Doesn't riding ability come into it?"

I thought for a moment. "The judges are looking for the perfect picture. Say you had a really wonderful actress but she wasn't very pretty, would she get work as a leading lady or would it be character parts."

"You're right. She'd be a character actress."

"Because no matter how fine an actress she is, she can't overcome the fact that she's not the most beautiful actress, too."

"It's no wonder you hated showing."

I remembered all the times when we entered the in-gate and felt like I had been set up for failure. It wasn't Butch's fault. It wasn't my fault. We both did the best we could do. When I was pushing myself as hard as possible and still that wasn't enough, it became an exercise in futility.

If I had asked for another horse, as Greer did, I probably would have gotten one, but then that would have been a betrayal of Butch. When he was diagnosed with arthritis and had reached the end of his career, then Butch could retire. It made sense. Then Lockie found CB for me.

Lockie, who changed everything here without trying. He changed me, Greer, my father and the farm, all in the same way he rode—by instinct. He was self-assured and confident but had little ego.

As the gate opened, and he entered on Roux, I exhaled. The knowledge that he was more than capable of riding this round lifted any concerns I usually had. We watched as they jumped what looked like enormous verticals. The triple combination down the diagonal with a wide oxer as the last element had caused problems for many. Lockie and Roux cleared it with no difficulty.

The audience applauded as they made it over the last fence, sponsored by a real estate agency, with wings shaped like mansions. Lockie let Roux canter an arc, then brought him back to a trot.

"He's lame," I said.

9

"The horse?" Jules asked. "How can you tell?"

"Right front leg," I replied.

If I saw it, I was sure Lockie felt it and a moment later, he dismounted quickly and went to the far side to check.

Roux hadn't hit a rail, so maybe he had landed poorly.

As Lockie led him from the arena, the lameness was more pronounced, and the announcer mentioned it. That was the end of the Orange Coast Classic for Roux.

"Will Lockie call?" Jules asked.

"In a couple hours, after all the veterinary assessments have been done. I should go back to the barn."

Greer entered from outside and Joly ran to her to be picked up for kisses and hugs.

"They're out on a trail ride. Three go out, and two come back. That's the logline for Mr. Smarmy Star's new movie.

He plays the detective who has to investigate how the child disappeared."

"Which one doesn't come back?"

"Ryan, of course. The other two throw her into a ravine."

Jules looked up. "We don't have a ravine here."

"Then they'll dig one in order to get rid of her." Greer put Joly on the floor and removed her jacket. "For such a cute kid, she really is a pain in the butt."

"There's good news. Sally Ebison is going to consider taking Ryan and Ding."

"Can she just take Ryan and leave the pony?"

"Yeah, he's a sweetheart, isn't he?" I replied. "Are you still coming to the show tomorrow?"

Greer shot me a look. "I said I would help, so I will, but boy, that was a bait and switch to beat all."

"Ryan was pretty well-behaved in Florida. I had no idea she was a miniaturized Adam Saunders. Have you read about this guy? He's like the Tasmanian Devil to work with. All demands all the time."

Jules stood and went to see if her cupcakes had cooled enough to frost. "That's normal for Hollywood. They all come to believe their own publicity."

"She's a little girl," I started.

"She's not that little. I was her age once," Greer interrupted.

Jules gave her a hug. "Were you?"

"I know all about being rude," Greer said. "I know all about being demanding. I learned these lessons from a master."

That was true. Victoria could be a horror.

"And she's coming up the walk now," Greer added looking out the kitchen window.

My head snapped around faster than Linda Blair's in *The Exorcist*. "What?"

The door opened.

"Bonjour!"

"What do you want," Greer said, then looked at me. "See how I can be rude?"

"Well done, you," I replied.

"Darling. I brought something for you."

"Beware of antiques bearing gifts," Greer commented.

Victoria nodded. "Nice play on words. It's so unfortunate you didn't want to finish school. You would have been brilliant."

"We're finishing next week," I said. "Early graduation."

Victoria laughed. "That correspondence course you two are doing? How lovely." She opened her large bag and removed a small box then held it out to her daughter.

Greer reached down and picked up Joly. "You don't have anything I want."

"Happy Valentine's Day."

"You're late."

"I wasn't in the country," Victoria said. "I was back home in England."

"You should have stayed."

"Not when I'm on my way to important meetings with agents in California."

I had the sound turned down on my laptop but the Classic was still in progress. Cam was scheduled to ride after the next two horses but I would not mention that to Greer.

"Why are you going to California, Ms. Rowe?" Jules asked as she picked up the dessert dishes and brought them to the counter.

"You know my book is number one," Victoria replied.

"In the muck and mire category?" Greer asked.

"Over all, darling."

We hadn't paid attention to *Tight Chaps and Loose Tarts* in weeks, hoping it would sink to the bottom and be forgotten.

Victoria pushed the box at Greer. "Will you please take it?"

Greer whipped the box from her mother's hand. "Happy?" She tossed it at me.

Opening the box, I removed a miniature, beautifully crafted gold high heel shoe, set with gold beads and semi-precious stones. Or I thought they were semi-precious and not rubies, emeralds and diamonds. I held it up.

"It's a pendant," Victoria said.

"Where am I supposed to wear it? The barn?"

"Get a boyfriend, have him take you to fabulous restaurants. Enjoy life. I did at your age," Victoria said then laughed. "I still do!"

"You don't have to deal with you," Greer commented. "That could be the explanation."

Victoria laughed, kissed the air by Greer, waved to the rest of us and paused at the door for dramatic effect. "You don't think that devastatingly handsome blond would play himself in the movie, do you?"

"Get the freak out of here!" Greer shouted.

I lowered the screen to my laptop because Cam's round was in progress.

"Would you like to come to LA with me?" Victoria asked.

Greer and Joly left the room.

"I suppose that's a no. You'll never have any fun in life, darling," Victoria called to her, "if you don't start saying yes." She gave us a bright smile. "Au revoir," she said and was gone.

"It must be French day in the provinces." I opened the lid, Cam's round was finished and there was no indication of the score. "Time to go back to the barn."

"Does she really have a movie deal?" Jules asked.

"Probably. We can always expect the worst from her."

I left the house and found the three girls just returning from their hack.

"It's too cold to stay out any longer," Gincy said.

Poppy glared at Ryan.

"I hope you girls had a nice ride," Aly said. "You have a lot of work to do before tomorrow morning."

The girls dismounted, and led the ponies into the barn.

"Aly," I said. "If Ryan gives you too much trouble, we can make other arrangements."

She smiled. "Poppy is a handful. I expect there to be arguments, fights over the bathroom, and complaints from both of them. Don't worry about it. I will treat Ryan the same as Poppy. She won't get special privileges and I expect complaints about that."

"It's only for a week and if we get lucky, a few days. I may have found a trainer for her closer to her school." I held up my crossed fingers. "Not that I'm superstitious."

***

We worked past dinnertime to braid the ponies and get Spare ready for Cap. Aly was going to bring Tango and Beau in her trailer. Pavel was going to drive the van with Call and Spare. The classes were all in the morning and I hoped we would be headed home by noon. I knew such expectations were often dashed on the rocks of reality.

133

Ryan waved from the back of the Beck's SUV and the girls were gone which was only a temporary relief. Another of my hopes was that Gincy and Poppy would take pity on me and behave so that I only had to deal with one prima donna. Ryan was not happy she was being compelled to ride a garish spotted pony when her perfect flaxen chestnut was in the barn, one hundred percent sound, and doing nothing but eating hay.

I felt sorry for her but not very.

By dinnertime, Greer had mostly recovered from Victoria's visit but we did spend about fifteen minutes trying to translate what she meant. Victoria had dropped so many hints that I was surprised there weren't dents in the floor.

If I had more energy for a useless project, I would have gotten on the Internet and tried to learn if a Hollywood studio did have interest in *Tight Chaps.* I didn't see how that was possible since who was interested in horse movies except horse people.

But the way her book was selling, there had to be an audience who was skipping over the horsey parts and concentrating on the guy who had certain physical attributes similar to that of a horse.

Cam could not possibly play him. That had been Greer's immediate fear as she had read the book, that Cam was the model for the playboy of the western hemisphere.

Was Victoria teasing about having been inspired by Cam? No. I believed she had been very taken with him and fortunately, Cam hadn't responded to her.

If Cam had flirted back, it probably would have resulted in three to five years at the Federal Correctional Institution for Greer.

She didn't seem to require getting talked down from a ledge, if we had one, so I got ready for bed. I was just drifting off to sleep when my phone rang.

I checked first. "Hi."

"Hi. Sorry I'm so late. We just got back from the veterinary clinic."

"It's serious then."

Lockie paused. "He won't be sound for the next few weeks."

"Pack up and come home."

"I have Counterpoint here and might as well finish what we started. Teche gave me another horse to ride called Maque Choux. He's trying to persuade me to stay on after the end of the month."

"What's he offering you?"

"A dark chili red Porsche. Oh, Talia, it's wonderful. He stopped at the car dealership on the way back to seduce me with it."

"What did you say?"

"That I have a pickup truck and can't drive two vehicles at the same time. There isn't anything I want except to come home."

I paused. "Don't be so sure of that."

"What happened now?"

I told him.

10

GREER AND I stood together near the bleachers with the other trainers as the ponies entered for the under saddle class. It was exactly as I had expected. Some ponies were woolly bears, others had been clipped. Some were braided, some were not. Some riders seemed to know what they were doing, others didn't have a clue.

I had told the Zuckerlumpens many times to stay away from other ponies. It was impossible to tell which one would kick, buck, run off, or behave like a lamb. Take a position on the track and stay there. Let the others circle in a desperate attempt to be seen by the judge.

Poppy was full of confidence. Gincy had less experience and knew it, so felt a bit unsure. Ryan had just come from the A show circuit in Florida and thought this was a gathering of backyard ponies, pulled in from the field that morning and shoved into the trailer with their morning hay hanging from their mouths. She was probably correct about that assessment for some of the riders.

This was a small schooling show in the middle of February. Ryan didn't understand that it was about gaining experience, not winning ribbons.

"Are you nervous?" Greer asked me.

"Shouldn't I be?"

"No. Accept that something ridiculous will happen that you have no control over and let it go."

"Are you trying to convince me that you weren't nervous riding against Nicole Boisvert?"

"No, I wasn't. I was focused on what I was doing."

The ponies were asked to canter. Poppy got off on the right lead immediately, Beau took a few trot strides before getting the canter and Call picked up the wrong lead. Ryan pulled him back, and asked again. He picked up the wrong lead. Then she was flustered and let her reins slip through her fingers.

"This is a pony who can do flying changes better than most of the horses in the barn. It's Ryan's fault," I said.

"I can explain this situation to you," Greer said as Ryan finally got herself organized enough to get the correct lead. "The kid's not a good rider. I saw it yesterday. She's fine on a push-button pony but when it comes to riding something that isn't so cooperative, she's lost."

"After all the years she's ridden and all the lessons she's had, Ryan can't ride a normal pony?"

Greer nodded. "Sad, isn't it?"

A moment later the ringmaster asked for the class to walk then reverse. One kid at the top of the ring was trying to do a turn on the haunches and was making a mess of it. Soon ponies were coming at her head-on and had to avoid her.

"This is what I meant," Greer said. "You can't do anything about it."

A young woman came up to us. "Hi, your assistant at the van said you'd be here wearing your stable colors. I'm Sally Ebison."

We shook hands. "I'm Talia Margolin, and this is my sister, Greer Swope."

"Which one is Ryan?"

"She's on the Appaloosa pony," Greer said.

Of course, at that moment Ryan was in the process of trying to get her canter leads correct again. I thought she was probably not being precise enough in her aids. Since I had ridden Call, I knew he was extremely well-trained and sensitive. If her legs weren't doing what they should, he would be trying to intuit what Ryan wanted from him. If that was the wrong lead, that was fine with him. Call was very cooperative.

The class was asked to walk and line up in front of the ringmaster. There was a wait of several minutes while the judge made her decisions and then the results were given to the announcer.

"We have the results of class 8, Pony Hunters Under Saddle. First place goes to number 47 Poppy Beck on Tango Pirate. Second place goes to number 48 Gincy Hamblett on Beau Peep."

There was polite applause as the girls rode forward to collect their ribbons and the announcer continued reading off the results. "Sixth place goes to number 126 Ryan Saunders on Calling All Comets."

We applauded as the ponies left the ring.

Ryan was in tears by the time we got outside. "If I was riding my pony, I would have won!"

Poppy was smiling as Aly came up to her. "Wasn't Tango great?"

"He floated across the dance floor," Aly replied.

The Hambletts congratulated Gincy and they all went back to the trailer.

Greer looked at Ryan. "Get a grip. It's not that big of a deal."

Ryan couldn't stop crying.

Maybe with that heightened sense of drama she would follow her father's footsteps into the same business.

Sally walked up to her. "Ryan, I'm Sally Ebison from Semple Hill Farm. Would you like to keep your pony there? It's close to your school."

Ryan cried harder. "You're kicking me out, too, Talia!"

I reached up and helped her off Call.

"We told you it was only temporary for you to stay at Bittersweet," Greer said. "It's too far from your school. You want to be near Ding, don't you?"

Ryan nodded. "Do I have to leave now?"

"Not if you don't want to. Stay the week like we planned," I said and silently begged Poppy to behave.

"You can visit Semple Hill and we can get to know each other better. If you think you'll be happy there, we'll get your pony for you. He'll have a comfy stall with a view." Sally really knew how to deal with a pony rider.

I felt better. Greer felt better. Ryan did not, yet, but maybe she would see that commuting from New York to Connecticut was a waste of time when Semple Hill was so nice as well as convenient.

***

We pulled out of the showgrounds just before noon with Poppy taking the pony hunter championship and Gincy taking reserve. Cap had two very nice, clean rounds on Spare and took the blue in both. There wasn't much competition so it really was more for experience than glory.

"It was a good day," Greer said.

"No one got trampled," I replied as she turned the truck into the driveway.

"Bittersweet Farm got positive attention and we found a new home for Ryan."

I sighed.

"Don't. You won't be going to shows very often. You'll want to go with Lockie, won't you?"

"Of course."

"In case, right?"

"Bite your tongue! Thoughts are like magnets!"

"Thoughts are ephemeral. If everything I ever thought would happen both good and bad actually occurred, I'd be living a very different life."

"A better life?"

"No, a different one."

We got out of the truck and went to the house where Jules had a large lunch in the last stages of completion waiting for us. Once everyone had taken care of their ponies, they'd join us for a celebratory meal. Not to celebrate winning but being together.

While Greer walked Joly, I filled Jules in on everything that had taken place and she listened intently.

"Ryan seems like a very sad little girl."

"Yes but so was I when I came here," I replied.

"You were with family. I know you didn't feel like it for a few years—"

"Right."

"—but eventually you all got on the same page. Who is there for Ryan to be on the same page with?"

"I don't know but why should it be us?"

"I'm not saying it should be."

"If she changed schools..." Jules started.

I froze. "Please don't say what I think you're going to."

"And went to The Briar School she could easily make the commute here."

"Her father, or mother, or guardian ad litem—"

"You're watching too much *Law and Order*," Jules said.

"Lockie said I shouldn't watch *House* anymore because he catches every disease they feature. Someone chose that school for her and didn't choose The Briar School which is well-known and well-respected. She should stay where she is. It's...familiar. It was very difficult for me to go from my old school to Briar."

Jules reached out and squeezed my arm. "I know, Dolcezza."

Greer came in with Joly and gave him a little bit of lunch, then we went upstairs to change.

"Lockie's class is streaming live this afternoon," I called to her.

"That new horse Mock Me Once Shame on You, Mock Me Twice Shame on Me?" Greer asked from her room.

"Maque Choux," I said.

Greer appeared in the doorway looking gorgeous in a pale striped shirt and trousers. "What's that?"

143

"Jules said it was a Cajun corn dish of some kind."

"With plenty of mouth-scorching spice on it."

"How could it not?"

We went downstairs followed by Joly who was having an easier time negotiating the stairs as he grew. Greer worked her artistry on the table, and soon everyone was up from the barn and we sat down to eat. For dessert there were cookies decorated with ribbons, trophies, and likenesses of all the ponies as close as it was possible to get with royal icing.

Jules gave each girl a portrait of her pony in a cellophane wrapper tied with a bow then everyone left.

"Phew." It was almost time for Lockie's class so I turned on the laptop as we cleaned up the dining room and kitchen, keeping an eye on the screen.

Just as we were finishing, the class started and there was a shot of the order the horses would go. Lockie was near the top of the list and Cam with his two rides for Teche was in the middle. That was good for Greer, who could leave the room or change and go to the barn to ride Citabria.

A few minutes later, I called everyone over as Lockie was entering the ring on a large dark bay horse. He made a large circle and headed for the first fence. The horse was a very powerful jumper and cleared it easily.

"There's such a sense of stillness about him," Jules remarked. "He's very centered. Rather unusual disposition."

"You mean compared to everyone else here," Greer said.

Jules laughed. "Yes, but it's not about control. He just doesn't get shaken by the small stuff."

"If you came as close to dying as he did, most of everything else seems to be small stuff," I replied.

"He didn't come close to dying," Greer countered.

"It could have gone either way that day and he was very lucky."

"Or he was meant to come here and become part of the family," Jules said.

Lockie had a clear round but came in over the fastest time. There were about forty more horses to go.

"I have things to do," Greer said, knowing Cam would be going in about fifteen minutes, and left the kitchen to go upstairs.

About ten minutes later, Greer came shrieking down the stairs. "Have you seen the Equestrian Elite site?"

"Why would I go there," I asked.

Greer spun the laptop around and opened another window to show us what had upset her.

There was a photo of Cam and Sloane Radclyffe in eveningwear attending the Napier Veterinary Hospital Valentine's Day Charity Gala.

I couldn't remember when Greer had been so upset, and I had seen her lose it many times in the past.

"Greer," Jules said. "Calm down. Tell us what the problem is."

She paced back and forth in the kitchen. "Sloane Radclyffe, the Scintillating Socialite?!"

"Should I know her?"

"Radclyffe Industries. Very wealthy."

Greer pointed to the screen as she strode past. "With all that money, she can't afford a good haircut?"

Jules looked closer. "It does look a bit unkempt."

"If you're going to wear an evening gown, you dress up for the occasion not down."

I was sure Greer knew the protocol.

"Will you look at her? She looks like she just got out of bed. And she probably did."

I tried to pull the computer away from her.

"Look at the caption!"

"'Cameron Rafferty, one of America's top show jumpers, is being considered for the lead role in the soon to be a major motion picture based on Victoria Kensington-Rowe's bestselling novel *Tight Chaps and Loose Tarts*,'" I read.

Frustration pushed her over the tipping point and tears welled up in Greer's eyes.

I understood. It was a body blow coming at her from two sides.

Never allowing anyone to see her cry, Greer ran up the stairs with Joly and Jules following her.

I reached for my cell phone and clicked on the speed dial.

"Do you know I'm riding in about five minutes?"

"Yes, Cam. This won't take long. Is there any possibility you can come home with Lockie on Monday?"

"Who will be here to ride the horses?"

"I know, but Greer saw the photo of you and Sloane. She read that you are going to be in her mother's movie."

"I accompanied Sloane and I'm not going to be in a movie."

"She's very upset."

There was silence at the other end. "Does she want to see me?"

"She needs to see you," I replied.

***

I knocked on Greer's door. "Are you doing something you shouldn't?"

"Beyond everything, no."

"May I come in?"

"Yes."

I went in and she was on the bed with Joly.

"Do you want to talk about it?"

"What good will that do?"

"Maybe you'll feel better."

Greer stroked Joly's head. "It would have been easier if you hadn't butted into my life."

147

"Cool. I should have known this was my fault."

"People used to like me."

"Did they?"

"At least there was the illusion they did."

"What changed?"

"I stopped being like them and started being like you. No one likes you."

I smiled.

"Now they don't like me."

"We love you." I took Greer's hand.

Tears flooded her eyes.

"The minute I wouldn't sleep with Cam, he went out and attached himself to someone else. The Scintillating Socialite! Why her?"

"I don't know. You could ask him."

"Highly unlikely!"

"Maybe they just attended the charity event together."

"You have no idea. I didn't tell you what it was like in Napier."

I handed her a tissue. "Were you protecting me?"

"Yes. It was like a frat party but with no college students."

I nodded.

"Don't worry about Lockie. He went to bed earlier than anyone else. By himself."

"Now that you're not there to tattle on him, maybe things have changed." I held back my smile.

"Highly doubtful."

"I know you're angry with Cam—"

"He wanted to sleep with me!" Greer shouted.

"I'm sure you have that effect on most men. Think of it as a compliment."

"Think of it as him wanting to use me."

"I'm not taking sides but I think you misinterpreted his gesture."

"I'm pretty good at interpreting these things. I lived on the Continent for quite a while."

"That's true," I replied. "He made a mistake. It was a hurtful one but you can't let it keep hurting you."

"Everything is so simple for you."

"Well, the advice is but the feelings are complicated. I struggle too, and you're right, no one did like me at The Briar School. You and your friends managed to disinclude me in all your activities. If there was no way around having me in your presence, Sabine mocked me mercilessly. Thank you for not joining in."

"Is this what shame feels like?" Greer asked as she swiped at the tears.

"You made a mistake, that's all."

"Why couldn't he like me for me?"

I squeezed Greer's hand. "Ask him."

"Are you crazy?"

"You'll have an answer. It will help you in the future."

"No."

"You will see Cam again. Are you planning on being somewhere else every time he's at the barn?"

"Good suggestion."

"Greer."

There was a pause of several minutes then she looked up from Joly. "You avoid people who have an agenda. Stay in control of the situation. You drive, not them. Then you're safe."

***

"This is a mess," I told Lockie later that night.

~ 11 ~

LOCKIE CALLED ME from the airport to say he and Cam were on the way and would be at the barn by late morning.

After telling Jules, I said "I don't know what to do."

"You already set this in motion," she replied.

"Was I wrong?"

"It doesn't matter now. Unless you warn Greer, she'll have to deal with him. That's what you wanted, isn't it?"

"Yes."

"Why?"

Jules was putting together a large pot of chick pea soup for lunch. Fortunately, she had all that experience in restaurants dealing with large numbers of people, otherwise we'd be eating in shifts, one day on, one day off. Ciabatta rolls were proofing in the oven and there was turkey breast for sandwiches.

"I don't want Greer to be in this much pain and if she doesn't resolve this soon, it will be like falling off over a scary jump. It will be progressively more difficult to conquer that fence. That's how I spent years. I had a couple bad falls and I couldn't go forward until Lockie and CB helped me. I'm trying to help Greer but I feel like I'm intruding. Maybe she doesn't need my help."

"It's a predicament, isn't it," Jules replied as she tipped the cutting board with the sliced mushrooms into the stockpot. "I'm just curious. Why did you think she needed to see him at all?"

I thought for a moment. "Because he understands her in a way the rest of us don't. I think that's why her reactions are so intense where he's involved. He's too close to the bone. Her behavior doesn't make sense otherwise."

"How did you get so smart?" Jules asked.

"None of it is me. My mother was a wise woman," I replied.

"All of it is you," Jules said.

It wasn't, I was quite certain of that. He who rides the tiger, cannot dismount, my mother said. Once you start a course of action, it must be followed to its conclusion.

I knew Greer would fire everything she had at Cam one day but it was impossible to predict which day it would be. I thought he could handle it. I hoped I was right.

***

My phone rang. It was Lockie.

"We just touched down at the airport so we'll see you in about an hour. Is the farm a hot zone?"

"She doesn't know, so what do you think?"

"I hope this doesn't involve spurting blood and sutures, is what I think," Lockie replied.

"See you."

"This is where I say bye, right?"

"Bye." I clicked off and turned to Jules. "We have another hour of peace and then let the fireworks begin."

"I think I have to do some shopping for dinner so you can take over the lunch service."

"No! Don't leave me here by myself!"

Jules smiled. "I wouldn't do that. Someone should be here with tourniquets and be ready to call the ambulance."

"This was a bad idea, wasn't it?"

"No. You are right."

I checked on the rolls. They were rising nicely and would be ready to put in the oven in about a half hour.

It really depended on how clever Cam was and how much he did care about Greer. If I had read him incorrectly, then this would be a fiasco.

After watching him ride for months, I thought Cam was smart, diplomatic, kind, and strong-willed. He wouldn't be succeeding in the jumper division if these traits were not a part of his character. I didn't know what Greer needed from him but I was willing to believe he knew.

If he didn't know, then somehow I would get Remington back for him and he could put all his horses at Acadiana Farm because Greer would make his life a living hell if he stayed at Bittersweet. Our lives would not be great either.

Jules and I finished preparing lunch and right on time, Lockie and Cam arrived.

"Hi," I said to them.

Lockie kissed me, then Cam kissed me.

"It's so cold up north," Cam said. "Luckily, I'm not going to be here long."

"When are you leaving?"

"Late tomorrow," he replied. "Someone has to be there to ride the horses. They can have today off and tomorrow they can be exercised but it's my job to prepare the horses for next weekend's show."

"Thank you for making the trip," I said.

"I should see my mom and grandfather so no matter what happens, it's not wasted."

Cam went to use the lavatory on the first floor while Lockie cleaned up at the kitchen sink.

The door opened and Greer entered. "Hi."

"Hi, Greer. I hear you had fun with the ponies yesterday," Lockie said while drying his hands on a towel.

"No one was trampled," I said.

"Ever the positive thinker," Greer replied. "Bittersweet students took the pony hunter championship and reserve so I think that's a good day."

"And you found a new home for Ryan."

"Yes. Bonus points for that," she said.

"Hi, Greer," Cam said as he stepped into the kitchen.

She went pale.

I'd heard that expression before but I had never seen it happen.

"What are you doing here?"

"All my horses live here."

"Get out."

"I'm going to have lunch. I'm going to ride Jetzt, then get on Deep Stack, Lockie and I will school Wing and Kyff and sometime late in the afternoon when I'm done with everything I need to do, I'll go home."

"Let's sit at the table and have lunch," Jules suggested as she brought the basket of rolls with her.

"Are you leaving?" Greer demanded.

"No," Cam replied as he sat down.

"Greer, you can sit in my place," I said.

"And then I have to look at him. No! If you won't go, I'll go."

Greer took three strides to the doorway, Cam stood grabbed her arm and pulled her out the kitchen door with her leaning against him the entire way, just like a horse unwilling to get into a trailer.

"Excuse us," he said.

The door slammed and they went around the back of the house where we couldn't see them anymore.

"Exciting." Lockie began to eat.

Jules told Lockie about the cooking show taping and asked if he would like to attend. He said yes, so we had that to look forward to if we didn't have to make visits to the hospital with flowers and hamburgers because of wounds that Cam and Greer incurred during this disagreement they were having.

We were half-way through lunch when the door opened and they entered.

Cam 1. Greer 0 by the look of them.

The point of this visit was not that she should be defeated and that he should be the victor. I had envisioned the possibility of something far more equitable and soothing. It was impossible to tell what had happened although there were no signs of blood. That Greer was completely silent was not usually a good sign, just like a volcano may be quiet before it erupts covering the countryside with molten lava.

Cam pulled out the chair for her and she sat. He sat next to her. "What's for lunch?"

156

***

Conversation was very limited during lunch and I was thrilled to go to the barn to get away from oppressive silence.

Greer went to her office to work with Amanda as she usually did, Cam and Lockie worked with Jetzt and Whiskey.

I mounted CB and we got away from the debris field. We went over the stream, through the woods, up the mountain and then back down the other side where we reached the dirt road, which brought us home.

I wanted Greer to be happy in her life. If not happy, at least comfortable. That day I wasn't sure it was possible. Her past was a swamp of creatures dark and slimy that clawed at her, of memories as sharp as the razors she had turned on herself.

Cam saw another Greer. Which one of us was right? Or was it both of us?

I found them in the indoor, Cam on McStudly, Lockie on Kyff and Cap acting as ground crew who was moving the cavellettis when needed. McStudly was being started and Kyff was being brought back to the beginning because Lockie was of the opinion that horses were rushed into work before they could handle what was being demanded of them.

Many trainers couldn't afford to take the time to let a horse grow into himself. Bittersweet could. We had ongoing expenses that had to be covered but rent or mortgage wasn't necessary. This was our home, bought and paid for long ago by my very prescient great-grandfather and we had all the time we needed.

CB and I watched until their session was over then we all left the arena. Greer was on Citabria, then Cam and she walked up the driveway together.

I slid off CB. "What's going on?"

Lockie dismounted from Kyff and ran up his stirrups. "I have no idea."

"She doesn't look happy."

"No, she doesn't." Lockie led Kyff into the barn. "Tal, could we have a moment?"

"Sure. Where?"

"At the carriage house."

"I'll meet you there."

I took care of CB, went up to the house and got a few pastries Jules had been experimenting with in preparation for her cooking show appearance, then drove to the carriage house. He was kneeling by the fireplace working with kindling and newspapers, so I went to the kitchen and put two mugs of water into the microwave.

"Are you going to tell me not to do that again?" I asked as I brought the mango mini-cakes in on plates.

Lockie stood. "No, I'm going to tell you that it's good to be home."

I put my arms around him. "There's a place right by your shoulder where my head fits so perfectly."

We stood there long after the microwave stopped dinging.

**

Greer went out to dinner with Cam, Jules informed us as we arrived at the table.

"What did she say?"

"Cam and I are going out," Jules said.

"Was she smiling," I asked.

"No."

"Did she dress well?" I asked, desperate for a hint.

"She was dressed to go out to dinner."

"Where are they going?"

"Tal," Jules said as she brought the food to the table, "I told you everything. I know it was minimal but she seemed to be in a state of shock."

"That's not good," Cap said. "That happened to me once. The world stops. Luckily, Mill was there." Cap

159

laughed. "Of course, he doesn't have much patience with that kind of emotional crisis. He's a push forward personality, that's why he's such a good polo player."

"Don't worry about her," Lockie said as he began eating.

"She could—"

"Greer is a walking hand grenade with the pin pulled."

"So are you saying we should just make sure we're out of the blast radius?" I asked.

"Something like that."

"Lockie—"

"If Greer's with Cam, she couldn't be in better hands."

"That puts my mind at rest," Jules said quickly to end that topic. "So who is going to New York with me tomorrow?"

✍ 12 ✍

LOCKIE PUT ANOTHER LOG ON THE FIRE, which meant we were going to be up for a while.

"I understand that you're concerned about Greer. I am, too. Let them work it out for themselves. They're making progress. They hacked together, now they're out to dinner."

"Or maybe Cam's throwing her in the river with her feet weighed down with a couple cinder blocks."

Lockie laughed.

"I think she really likes him," I said.

"How odd is that. I think he really likes her."

"It hurt her so much to believe Cam only wanted to have sex with her. Rui came here and used her. Derry came here and used her. I'm sure those aren't the only two times."

"I'm sure."

"You know what Victoria's like. You know what she wrote in that disgusting book. This is the kind of atmosphere Greer was raised in. No wonder she was confused. She just wants to be appreciated for herself."

"Yes."

"Then Cam came along and, what, didn't explain himself well?"

Lockie squeezed my hand. "I'm so glad I'm home."

"You missed the high drama?"

He thought for a moment. "I miss people checking on me during the day not because you have nothing else to do but because you all care about each other so much."

I kissed his cheek.

"I love the way everyone here does hand-to-hand combat with life. This family is so different."

"From yours?"

Lockie shrugged. "Sure, from mine. From everyone. Most people are wrapped up in acquiring the baubles of the world and never understand what they're neglecting."

"You're not like that."

"I once was. You become very goal oriented on the circuit, the wrong goals, maybe. Your best angels leave and you're left to your own navigational abilities."

"Your instincts are good."

"Remember what I said once. Every horse is a good horse in the right place."

I nodded.

"That suggests he was a bad horse until he got to the right place."

"Maybe he was just a confused horse who didn't understand what was expected of him," I said.

Lockie paused for a very long moment. "You are why I'm in the right place now."

***

We got the chores done early and dressed for the trip to the city. Greer decided she had too much work to do for the Ambassador of Good Cheer so passed.

I didn't think the excuse was true but gave her high marks for knowing she wouldn't be good company. Since she was often not very good company anyway, I saw this as a bizarre sort of progress.

Lockie slept most of the way in the backseat while Jules and I discussed the show. She had spent hours on the phone with Gram determining just what needed to be done and how.

Of course, it seemed like a surprise on television, but the chefs were notified well in advance of what they'd be working with. Jules was assigned the dessert course because she was such a brilliant pastry chef. I agreed. Perhaps Gram had been, too, before he went vegan and served people ornamental grasses with a garnish of lip-puckering sour green plums.

Jules parked in the garage near the studio and we walked to the large building. At the doorway, she hugged us both. "Thank you so much for coming with me."

"You needed a cheering section," I replied, "and now you have one."

We were shown where to go and my father and grandparents had arrived a few minutes before and were waiting in the green room with the rest of the gallery. With a wave, Jules left to have a meeting of the minds with Gram and we sampled the goodies on a table meant for us.

My grandmother grilled me relentlessly about Greer and why she didn't accompany us. The concocted excuse wasn't convincing anyone.

Lockie thought it was good for them to be at the farm without the rest of us, although they'd hardly be alone. Maybe that wasn't the point of staying home. Maybe Cam would ride the horses, go to Acadiana to check on the youngsters who didn't make the trip to Florida, and then return home to spend time with his mother.

About an hour later, we were herded into the studio. By the look on Jules's face, I knew something was wrong.

The format of the show was to simulate the kitchen of a top restaurant at the height of the dinner rush, and the dishes prepared would then be dissected, and graded by the best-rated chefs. It was Gram, Jules and two other assistants against Vico Pyne and his team.

The twist was that at the last moment, the teams would be given a surprise for which they could not prepare.

It was quite apparent that Ludovico Pyne was a meat-eater. He was a large bodied man, not squidgy around the edges at all, and covered the studio floor with his bold strides like a predator. This was serious to him.

From everything I had heard and seen, it was an unreality show. While the viewing audience was assured nothing had been scripted in advance, it was only possible to believe that if Monday night wrestling was perceived to be an actual athletic competition.

My father leaned over his parents to me. "Have the winners been decided in advance?"

He was so smart to have picked up on the phoniness. "Not that I've heard," I replied, but it often seemed that way to me.

If it was about challenging a famous chef, how would it look if Joe Nobody won? Nobody could win once in a while just to prove it could happen but it couldn't happen all the time or the great chef wouldn't keep looking great.

Vico Pyne, we rubes from the country were told, owned the award winning Pyne's and there was a six week wait to get a table. You could get pretty hungry in that length of time and even cardboard would taste yummy by then.

"The other chef seems grumpy," my grandmother commented. "Maybe he should go vegetarian for a while."

I laughed.

"That Gram is a very calm young man," my grandmother replied.

"So much so that he could be asleep," my grandfather said.

The announcer walked over to stand in front of the gallery and explained how the taping would proceed. As much as possible, they would shoot the show straight through from beginning to end. Only if there was a fire or something exploded would they stop. It was fine for us to applaud but cheers should be reserved until the winner was revealed.

We were given some further guidelines to follow and then the announcer walked away.

"If Jules wasn't here, this would not be worth it," I said and everyone agreed.

The show began and this time the surprise set-back was that the teams had to change sides. For a moment, everyone was stunned. This was far more difficult than anyone had imagined and no one moved. Vico was the first to begin shouting for Gram's team to take their places at his work stations. He put Jules on the one next to his.

Gram tried to organize his new troops but got off on the wrong foot. Vico didn't have a wrong foot and forged quickly ahead. Of course, he had been in one of these challenges before and knew exactly what needed to be done.

Vico shouted, strode and used a knife so expertly that the blade looked like a silvery blur. He seemed to be everywhere at once. His dishes came together quickly, and loudly, while Gram struggled.

The announcer commented on all the supposed action, making it seem far more exciting that it actually was. What was more interesting was to see how easily Jules adapted to working with Vico while Gram became progressively more disorganized. I had all the confidence in the world for her. If Jules could handle us, this competition was a piece of cake.

Lockie leaned over and whispered in my ear, "Having fun?"

"Fun, no," I whispered back.

"Why are we here?" Lockie asked.

"Because of Jules," I replied.

Lockie smiled then brushed his lips against my cheek and I squeezed his hand.

We went back to watching the show and about two hours later, all the cooking was over, the judging began. Gram was lost as he attempted to describe his plates, and Vico Pyne was very self-assured as he colorfully described his.

"I think we have a winner," my grandfather commented.

"I would say so," my father agreed. "It wasn't much of a contest."

"If Jules had been in control instead of being the assistant—"

"Yes," my father said, "we would have a different outcome."

"Gram was lost without his grass clippings," my grandmother said with a wink.

"We just don't have palates refined enough to appreciate herbaceous borders," I replied.

"Salamander eggs on a hammock of edible leaves," Lockie suggested.

"We can't take us anywhere," I laughed.

The winner was announced, and it was Vico as expected. We all applauded politely. He shook hands with Gram and gave Jules a lengthy hug then a kiss on each cheek.

I looked at Lockie.

"Does he know her?" my grandmother asked.

"Apparently," I said.

"Or she should give him a hard right to the solar plexus," Lockie added.

I had never heard of Vico Pyne until today. I wasn't even sure Jules knew the name of the chef they would be competing against. It was obvious that Jules and Vico had some sort of history and it was probably that they had worked in the same restaurant after she had finished her culinary training.

The audience was ushered to the floor where we could meet all the chefs and sample the dishes. Vico approached us with his hand at the small of Jules's back.

That convinced me that they knew each other, not just worked together in a kitchen.

Jules introduced each of us in turn and Vico shook our hands with a broad smile on his face.

"So Jules is a private chef for you now?"

"Yes," I replied. "We couldn't do without her."

"You could find another chef," Vico said. "They graduate by the hundreds every year."

There was something I didn't like about him. Perhaps it was that Vico was standing too close to her. Or that he still had his hand on her back, long past the time when it was necessary. Or that he suggested so casually that she could be replaced by a stranger.

Jules wasn't our chef, we all thought of her as part of the family even if she had her own family in California. Bittersweet Farm was a job but she never treated it as such, and always treated us like family, referring to us that way.

I had been worried about Gram the Extreme Vegetarian but now that Vico was in front of us, it was all too easy to wonder if there were moments when Jules did think she should have her own restaurant here or in Los Angeles.

"We need to get home," Jules said to Vico. "Our friend is flying back to Florida later today and we should say goodbye."

"Are you certain you must leave?" he asked.

"Quite sure." Jules untied the apron she wore around her waist.

"You could have dinner at Pyne at the chef's table."

"That would be lovely but there would be no way for Lockie and Talia to get home since I drove the car."

"They could drive and I'll see you get back tomorrow."

Jules smiled pleasantly. "That's such a lovely idea but I have a dinner service at the farm on my schedule."

He kissed her cheek. "Come down from the hinterlands and have dinner with me soon, Julietta."

I groaned softly and got a nudge in the ribs from Lockie.

"Let's go home," my father said and led the way out of the studio.

***

About halfway back to Connecticut, most of it in silence, I decided I'd had enough. "Are you going to tell us about Vico Pyne?"

"He's the reason I left the restaurant world and wound up at Bittersweet Farm."

Lockie started bumping the back of my seat so I wouldn't go any further.

"He's charming and cruel," Jules continued.

170

"I'm sorry."

"I'm not. It brought me to you."

Jules turned her head and smiled at me. The same smile I had come to treasure.

***

By the time we reached the farm, Cam had already returned to Florida. Cap told us his ride left earlier than expected. Greer had gone to town and no one knew when she was expected back.

Cap had worked with the Zuckerlumpens and let them pop over the low fences on the cross-country course. That had upset Ryan since she had never ridden over an outside course before. She insisted Ding couldn't do it with the snow and the footing wasn't good enough for him. The result was that the other two girls had a blast and Ryan sat out the fun on her pony hunter who couldn't be allowed to jump except in a ring.

The point of the hunter division had been to show horses who were used for hunting. This didn't seem to be true any longer but it made sense if the pony cost as much as every other horse in town.

I changed and went back to the barn to ride with Lockie. After a brief discussion, we decided to hack CB and Kyff out through the fields and into the woods.

"Cam and I talked about Deep Stack. We didn't know he was going to be a problem for you, so we'll find a buyer for him," Lockie said as we splashed across the stream.

"We are getting used to him."

"If that's true, is there any objection to hanging onto him for another month and put some weight on him?"

"Sure."

"You know what the old-timers used to say. Fat's the best color."

"He is lean. I'm just concerned that some enchanted evening he will see a Zuckerlumpen and squish!"

Lockie laughed. "That's legit. He belongs at a barn where there aren't little girls who want to put earrings on him."

"You'll be here fulltime soon so you'll be able to take complete control of his training and handling."

"I will."

"You know Greer and I have that high school test tomorrow."

"All right. There are plenty of horses for me to ride. I'm leaving on Thursday because I have a couple classes for Teche on Friday."

We rode along the path that twisted through the woods, fresh snow covering the ground. This was not the usual direction I chose, because Pavel had not yet been out there with his chain saw. There were many low hanging limbs and branches reaching out to snap one's face.

"Cam has really been decent about taking over for you during the week," I said.

"He is one of the good guys," Lockie admitted.

"I shouldn't worry about Cam and Greer then?"

"No."

I didn't say anything.

"Tal. Let them work it out privately."

"We don't have any privacy and we manage."

"We have the carriage house."

I nodded. "Yeah, I forgot about that."

"This really is between them."

It was getting dark so we turned for home.

***

Leaving Lockie in the barn, I went to the house to help Jules although she certainly didn't need it, but she had been cooking most of the day already.

After washing up, I checked the pots on the stove. "What can I do to help?"

"I think we're good. We don't have a full house tonight since you father is leaving for a business trip in the morning

173

and your grandparents will be staying in the city until he returns."

"About Vico," I started.

"Yes?"

"I know you had a life before us but I didn't expect to be confronted by it."

"I was surprised to see him, too." Jules diced mushrooms and placed them in a sauté pan.

"It's none of my business."

"What would you like me to tell you?"

"That you won't leave us," I replied.

"I will stay as long as you want me."

I thought for a moment. "Is that a trick answer?"

"How could it be?"

"Did you ever see that movie *Nanny McPhee*? The nanny says she'll stay if they need her but not if they want her. Something like that."

"So you don't actually know what Nanny McPhee said but I need to not say that if you're not going to be plagued by it."

"That's right."

"One day, Dolcezza, you will not need me or want me and then I must go. It's rather sad really but true."

"You did see the movie!"

"Yes." Jules laughed. "I knew someone who worked on the costumes for it." She stirred the vegetables in the pan. "What concerns you, Tal?"

"Don't you want a family of your own?"

"Yes, someday, but Vico cured me for the time being."

"I want you to be happy."

"I'm where I want to be." She hugged me. "More importantly, I was put here for a reason. Now go round up the others so we can eat."

Greer hadn't gotten home yet.

***

A cold front had come through that evening and the rain that had started after chores were done, had begun freezing on all that it touched. Lockie did the farm accounts for an hour while I watched the fire die down, then he turned off the light and joined me on the sofa.

"Do you still want me to show CB?"

"If you would like him to be your dressage horse, I have no objection. I don't speak for him, though."

Lockie watched the flames twist lazily upward in the fireplace. "It's surprisingly hard to give up everything."

"Only cross-country. You still have the show jumping and you can always do dressage."

He kissed me. "I liked the challenge of the three phases. They each have different requirements so the horse and rider must learn to be flexible, and fit. I'm less fit now than I was at Ruhlmann's."

"You can't be serious."

"It's much more physically demanding to ride several miles cross-country at speed than to show jump only. I'll have to change my slothful ways after Florida."

He was teasing, I knew that, but wondered if he still missed eventing.

"What if you didn't compete but just trained event riders?"

"Who would that be?" Lockie asked.

"Freddi has been at the lower levels around here for a few years. I'm sure she would love to get more serious. I know it's not where you were, but if you really miss it..."

"Who would she ride?"

I thought about it for a moment. The only real event horse in the barn was Wing and I had been transitioning him into the hunter division. "Tyr, Rosemary's horse. He's still here and Rosemary is still on her round-the-world junket."

"It's a tempting idea, Tal, but it is possible to try to do too much. That isn't fair to anyone. Maybe I can help her a little but not to the detriment of our other programs."

"I don't want you to feel that you're missing out."

Lockie put his arm around my shoulders. "I don't. Visiting the television studio seems to have made a big impression on you."

"It made me realize other people have aspirations I don't dream of."

"I'm surprised you would say that. You do so much here. You rescued CB, Remington, Wingspread and Call. You're training a new generation of riders to have a sensitivity for what their horses need. I know you think it's not enough, but if you want to make big changes you wind up taking little steps."

I rested my head on his shoulder and Lockie kissed the top of my head.

∽ 13 ∽

"I DON'T WANT TO INTRUDE," I began the next morning.

"Phut," was Greer's reply.

"You didn't come home until after I went to the carriage house. I'm concerned about you."

"Tal." Greer was exasperated with me.

We went into the dining room where the test was to be given. This was in case we ever wanted to attend college. Neither of us did, but perhaps in the not foreseeable future we would change our minds.

Sitting at my place, I took out my fountain pen. "Okay. I'll leave you alone."

I thought we had made progress over the last few months but maybe the experiences this year caused her to feel she didn't want to trust anyone including me.

Greer sat at the head of the table so we would not be in each other's line of sight.

Amanda entered, put the printed tests on the table while telling us how much time we had to complete them, and said that there would be no talking.

"Let us get on with it," Greer said.

Opening to the first page, I was nearly overcome with the reluctance to continue. I kept repeating to myself "This is the last time." Never in my life would I be forced to take another idiotic test. Instead of aiming for a B, I began thinking if I could get a D that was plenty.

About a half hour in, Greer put down her pen.

"When we lived in the South of France, my mother left me alone most of the time. I went to the cinema. I saw old French films because she didn't give me much money and matinees were cheap. It didn't occur to her there was nowhere for me to go and nothing to do. I saw every movie that I could. Last night I went to the Thaden Theater because they were showing *Un Homme et Une Femme* which I saw that summer. I always wanted to be like Anouk Aimée. Not only as Anne Gauthier, the character, but as Anouk." Greer laughed mirthlessly at herself. "I'm blonde. I'm English."

I said nothing.

"You look like her. You're so beautiful."

I replaced the cap for my pen so the nib wouldn't dry out.

"How could Dad avoid falling in love with your mother? She was so much like Anne Gauthier. When I saw her..." Greer paused for several minutes. "That summer my mother acquired a new boyfriend. Guy Saulnier. He came from a good family, moved on the fringe of the right circles. He was...handsome, dissipated in the way that certain French men become when they age. But fun. Energetic. My mother likes that. That's why she became bored with Dad. He's not fun. He doesn't sparkle.

"My mother would be off with her girlfriends to go shopping or wherever they went during the day and Guy and I would go to the beach, or take a road trip. He would show me the Roman ruins. We would have lunch in a little bistro where he would teach me about French food. Fois gras. Cassoulet. Pastries. I was well fed.

"I was like his girlfriend. He was patient. He started slowly. A caress here. A touch there. A hug goodbye. A kiss hello. *Bon amis*. He masturbated against my leg with his zipper up at first. It's what friends do for each other, *non*? If you want to be liked, you accept certain conditions. Quid pro quo."

I drew in a breath to speak.

"No, it's true. Everywhere." Greer smiled. "Then he unfurled himself. No underwear for Guy. Just this French sausage slipping against my leg until he was done. I was sticky most of the summer. Then he had enough or my mother had enough. Maybe Dad stopped sending money.

180

We went back to England and I was sent to a public school that was like a prison. I rarely left. Then I don't know what threat Dad issued but he pried me loose and I came here. I hated it desperately. *J'étais désolé.*"

"Greer..."

"You do half the test and I'll do the other half."

I shrugged. Whatever.

"Don't tell Dad."

"How long are you going to keep it a secret?" I shouted.

"However long I want," Greer shouted back. "It would still be a secret if freaking Cameron Rafferty hadn't butted into my life."

"He did you a favor!"

"This is a favor?"

"He was more concerned about you than ol' Guy was!"

Amanda entered the room. "No talking."

Standing, regally, with great comportment I could never manage, Greer ripped up the test and walked out.

I picked up my pen and stood. "Sorry."

Fortunately, Jules was out shopping, so I made it through the kitchen with no need for explanation and found Lockie at the barn dismounting from Kyff.

"That was fast."

"We scratched."

He ran up his stirrups. "What does that mean?"

"Lockie, please. Stop."

He turned toward me. "What happened?"

"We were thirty minutes into the test and she started telling me about living in the south of France and how her mother's boyfriend molested her for a summer."

Lockie nodded.

"Did Cam tell you?"

"He didn't need to. I didn't know the specifics but I could guess."

"Is she right and this is happening everywhere and I'm too dumb to know it?"

Lockie reached out and pulled me to him. "You're not dumb. You're not naïve. Well, maybe a little. It's comes from that wonderful instinct you have to think well of people."

"Fantasyland."

"Better that than the gutter."

"Does my father suspect?"

"I don't know."

"Does Victoria know?"

"I don't know that either."

I held him tightly.

"If you hold me any closer, you'll be behind me," he teased. "What do you want to do?"

"Help her."

"She doesn't want it right now. Spot me on Wing and then we'll have lunch."

***

Jules had a large celebratory lunch prepared for us and hugged me as I entered the kitchen. "Congratulations, my new graduate! Where's my other new graduate?"

What followed was a silence you only experience in deep space.

"Why are you making that 'don't go there' face at me, Lockie?" Jules asked.

I squirted soap on my hands at the sink and began to run the water. It was standard procedure to wash up before handling food even if we cleaned up at the barn. "We had a little problem with the test."

Jules handed me a towel.

"We didn't finish it. Surprisingly few words were exchanged regarding that part of the morning."

"Which must account for why Amanda isn't here."

"That's right," I said. "Have you seen Greer?"

"No. Nor Joly either."

"I'll go upstairs and check on her."

Jules offered me a half sheet pan to use as a shield. "Just in case."

"I may regret this but no."

Leaving the kitchen, I went up the stairs and to her door. I tapped.

183

There was a thud as something hit the door.

"Good aim," I said. "I have a wild arm, sometimes things I throw wind up behind me."

Thud.

"No wonder you were on the tennis team. You have a good eye."

"Go away."

"It's time for lunch."

"I'm not hungry!"

"Then be with the family and keep us company."

"Shut up!"

Back to that.

"Greer, open the door."

"No."

"Are you going to stay in your bedroom for the rest of your life?"

"The rest of your lives!"

"Wait. We need to die before you come out?"

There was silence.

"Send out Joly because it's his lunchtime and I'll take him for a walk."

There were footsteps, the door opened enough for Joly to fit through, and I picked him up.

"Thank you," I said.

The door swung open the rest of the way and Greer turned back to her bed.

"What am I going to do if I don't see you for the rest of my life?"

"You'll get over it."

"I'm so good at getting over loss as demonstrated by my inability to get past losing my mother."

"You can have mine." Greer dropped onto the bed.

"That's very generous of you and hope you will not be offended if I pass."

Greer wouldn't look at me.

I sat on the edge of the bed with Joly. "What is so terrible about me knowing?"

"You'll feel sorry for me."

"That's true."

"I don't want to be pathetic."

"That's the last thing anyone would say about you."

Greer glared at me. "You wouldn't say it to my face. Behind my back, you would."

"My mother taught me not to gossip about anyone because it's so hurtful. It was nothing you could control."

"Stop! Of course it was. I could have told anyone. Although I'm not sure it would have done much good there. I could have called Dad."

"Why didn't you," I asked.

"Someone was paying attention to me. Someone liked me. I said it was a trade-off."

"That's in the past. We love you now and there's no trade-off with us. Some come downstairs and have lunch."

"No."

"We've all had bad things happen to us. You're not remarkable in the pain you suffered. Jules had a bad boyfriend just before she came here. I think she was getting the hell out of Dodge by the sound of it."

"I don't want you looking at me."

"Wear a Halloween mask then. You do remarkable work with the Ambassador of Good Cheer. You're so well organized and have terrific ideas for publicity that will grow the program. I teach two little girls how to post on the correct diagonal."

"We couldn't even finish the GED."

"Nope."

"I was supposed to go to Oxford."

"Well, la-di-da."

"Will Dad be angry with us?"

"Put one of your beautiful dresses on, smile and say you had a melt-down. Blame it on me, I don't care. He's given up trying to herd us and he's so damn impressed with what you've done, the piece of paper that, may I remind you, we don't really need, is insignificant to him."

"Are you sure?"

I nodded. "Very sure. Wash your face. Comb your hair and come downstairs to prove you love us as much as we love you."

"Okay but I'm never going to be in the same room with Cam again."

I argued with myself. Should I ask why not? Should I let it go? "Why not?" I couldn't help myself.

"He knows all my secrets," Greer said from the bathroom.

"Not by a long shot."

We went downstairs and Greer worked her usual magic on the table while Cap and I helped Jules with the food. Lockie came up from the barn and we sat down to eat.

"There's a show at Twisted Oak Farm the first week of March," Cap began. "I think Spare could benefit from entering a few classes. Would that be okay?"

"You don't have to ask permission," I said.

Cap looked to Lockie. "Do you think he's ready for another show? Maybe you want to work with him."

"Have Greer help you," Lockie said as he reached for Jules's homemade bread and butter pickles.

I held my breath.

Greer took a moment then nodded. "Consider him yours for as long as you're here."

"Thank you, Greer," Cap said. "I think Spare's terrific and I'll do my best with him."

***

We all went to the barn after lunch and without saying anything, Greer tacked Citabria and left the yard.

"Cap get on Spare while we have a half hour and I'll have a look at where you are," Lockie said. "You must be doing something right to have won the championship at the last show."

Walking past him, carrying her saddle and the bridle over her shoulder, she laughed. "There wasn't a lot of competition."

"That's fine. Tal, would you get on Kyff and ride him around the indoor, too?"

"Are we working?" I asked heading for the tack room.

"I want to see what he looks like with you on him."

"Okay."

"When's the last time he misbehaved with you?"

I picked up my tack and returned to the aisle without answering.

"Does that mean he hasn't thrown a Kyffy Fit with you?" Lockie asked.

"Right. I asked him please not to."

Lockie laughed. "That's a novel approach to training. I should try it."

I led CB outside and Lockie's phone rang. "Just get on and warm him up, I'll be right there."

We went to the indoor and Cap was already trotting Spare on the track. He traveled in a perfect frame with her, bending into the corners, light on the forehand with a nice, long stride.

Like Butch, Bijou was a wonderful companion but he had taken Cap as far as he could. Now that she had a horse with other talents, it was obvious what a good rider she was. I was sure she had learned a great deal about training from working with the polo ponies but it was unfortunate, in a way, that she hadn't been able to work on her own substantial talents.

I asked Kyff to trot and went around on light contact with his mouth. At the top of the ring, we did a volte and I gave him a pat because it was very close to twenty meters. Perhaps my eye was improving. He walked and then cantered. His way of going was quite different from CB. Kyff was flatter, not downhill, but CB was always more on his haunches due to the intensive dressage training.

It was easy to understand why Kyff had been marked as a hunter but there was no reason why he couldn't do some exercises to shift his weight to the rear a little more. If he would go along with a different program. I was never quite sure what he would accept.

Lockie had entered the ring as I was riding away from him. "Nice, Cap. Sit back a little if you feel he's getting strong. That's it. Tal would you come here, please."

I sat and Kyff walked. We went to the center of the arena.

"Tal..."

189

"That bad?" I let the reins drop and Kyff stretched out his neck.

"Excuse me?"

I sighed. "I guess I need you on the ground. I don't ask much from him, trying to intuit what's going on in his head." I reached forward and gave him a pat near his ears. "Hello, in there. I can get off and you can ride him." I kicked free of my stirrups.

"Bend down."

I leaned over and Lockie kissed me.

"Was the phone call bad news? What aren't you telling me?"

"I'm not telling you anything because you're busy telling me what you're doing wrong and I'm trying to tell you how good you're doing with Kyff."

That didn't sound right. "Really?"

"Really. He looks terrific. I hope he'll be that good for me."

"Give him oatmeal cookies," I said. "That's my secret weapon."

"Is it okay if I believe it's more than that?"

I pushed my feet back into the irons. "What more could it be?"

"He thinks you're on his side."

"I am."

"It's not about riding. You have a gift, Tal." Lockie said. "Don't make a face at me. I know exactly how the horses feel. I want to be near you, too."

"Don't go back to Florida," I replied.

Lockie laughed. "Go out on the track and push him a little. Use your inside leg on him and a little inside rein, maintaining contact with the outside rein and see what happens."

"Do you want me to do a shoulder-in?"

"That's too much. Just let him feel your leg, then move it away. Sitting trot."

We trotted a few strides, I put my leg against the girth, trotted a few more strides, then removed contact.

"Like that?"

"Exactly."

"Nothing happened."

"He's getting ready to go back to work," Lockie said.

"Are you going to give me something to work on while you're away?"

"No. Do exactly what you've been doing and next month we'll see where we are. Caprice. Trot Mr. Lyric Line over the cavalettis. Don't let him get strong but don't fight. He'll get the idea on his own if you're always there to stabilize him."

"Talia, take Kyffhäuser for a drink of water at the stream and come back in time for your Zuckerwuerfel."

"You do find it necessary to use the proper German, don't you?"

"Jah."

"See you," I said as we left the ring and Lockie began to work with Cap.

Unintentionally, I caught up with Greer hacking on the road.

"Do you want me to go away?"

She shrugged.

"Kyff was good today. He was a lunatic in Florida, running around the ring squealing after dumping Nicole."

"Are you ever going to trust him?"

"That's a good question. It'll take a while. He'll have to prove he's trustworthy. Kyff was dangerous that day because whatever thought-process he has stopped working."

"They're all about flight, not fight."

"That's when they're the most dangerous to humans but I don't think he cared what happened to himself. That troubles me. Flight is about self-preservation."

"He could have jumped into the seating section but he didn't," Greer pointed out. If he really wanted to get out, there was an entrance. He had to remember where that was."

"Yes, if he was able to think and remember. I don't know what set him off."

"What did Nicole do to him?"

I rubbed his neck. "Nothing. They were jumping the course."

"Nobody has such strong reactions unless it's been building for a while." Greer snapped her fingers. "Then there's a trigger incident and it all comes out."

I nodded.

"Don't make it about me."

I smiled.

"So now that we're high school drop-outs, what do we do with our lives?"

"We more than finished high school."

"We could try to take the test again."

"No thanks."

"Me neither."

"I like how my life is now but don't have aspirations to greatness the way other people do. I'm a...support system. I'll help Lockie and you and the Zuckerlumpens. My mother told me to do what's in front of you. Do it to the best of your abilities."

We rode in silence for a while.

"My mother was a great woman. She touched many people and had a positive influence on their lives, but the world didn't know who she was."

Greer turned to me. "Maybe she could have done more if she had gone out into the world."

"We don't know that, do we? I suspect we don't have as much choice as we imagine. My mother was very effective where she was. Dad is our front man, going out into the world to affect change. That's the way I see it. Now you. Maybe you inherited that from him. I think you will do wonderful things that surprise everyone."

"I've always done things that have surprised everyone," Greer replied grimly.

"Today, for instance!"

Greer thought for a moment. "I don't want to alienate Amanda. I need her help to learn how to run a charitable organization."

"Who's her boss?"

"Dad."

"In the business world, how are his people skills?"

Greer's lips turned up at the corner just enough for me to detect a possible smile.

"She's used to it," I assured her as we turned down the driveway.

The Zuckerlumpens were just mounting their ponies with Cap helping and Lockie standing nearby.

"Do you need any help," Greer asked as she dismounted.

"With the ponies? I'd love it!" I handed Kyff's reins to Cap and followed the ponies into the arena with Lockie tagging along.

He stopped me by touching my hand. "Tal."

"What?"

"I can count on you."

"Of course."

"It wasn't a question."

I smiled. "Come help with the Zucker...verfens. They already have a crush on you."

"Zuckerwuerfel."

"They like Cam a real lot, too. At their age—fickle."

"At your age?"

"You know me. The original Klingon."

The girls were warming up and I stepped to the side to talk to Aly. I wanted to know how Ryan was faring with the Beck family and learned she was doing better than expected.

By the time I turned around, all activity had ceased and the girls were asking Lockie what it was like to ride at the National.

I watched him for a moment, in all his beautiful elegance, smiling at the Zuckerlumpens, teasing them as they giggled while he positioned their feet perfectly in their irons.

Greer linked her arm through mine and pulled me into the ring. "Don't cry. I did enough of that for both of us today, Tal."

I shook my head.

"I'll go get Call and ride in with them."

"You said you'd help me."

"As though you need help," Greer said.

"But, I do," I replied.

"Then let's work them until their little legs are shaking." Greer strode to the center. "Is everyone ready to work?"

"That's my cue to leave," Lockie replied. "I'll see you later, ladies."

The Zuckerlumpens groaned. Sometimes Ryan did act her age.

***

The whole lot of us went up to the house for tea and pastries and Jules greeted me at the door.

"Look who we have as company," she said.

I saw a man in the kitchen. "Who?"

Ryan ran past me. "Dad!"

He picked her up and they hugged.

Gincy and Poppy squealed in delight as Aly tried to calm them down.

"It must be Adam Saunders," I said to Greer.

"Must be," she replied.

"What are you doing here, Dad? Here, in Newbury. Did you come to get me?" Ryan asked as her father put her on the floor.

"I'm here on business."

I glanced to Jules and knew in an instant this was not good.

"Are you going to make a movie here?" Gincy asked.

"Can we be in it?" Poppy asked.

"Shhh," Aly said.

"I'm having a meeting with some agents and a writer who lives here. I may be starring in the film version of her book *Tight Chaps*."

Greer slapped her leg, Joly ran up to her, and they went out the door.

I took the phone out of my pocket and closed myself into the pantry.

"Talia, come out," Lockie said.

I clicked on Cam's number. It rang twice.

"What now?"

"Are you two still talking?"

"No."

"I know she never wants to see you again but seriously she wanted me dead a couple hours ago and forgot that, too."

There was a long pause. "What happened?"

"Everything. We were talking the GED and she told me what happened in France. We didn't finish the test, she tore it up and left. She wasn't going to come out of her room until we all died so we wouldn't look on her with pity. We hacked and she got past that. Now we came in from the barn and Adam Saunders might be playing you in the movie."

197

"Shoot her full of Ace Promazine and she'll be fine in the morning."

"Cam. We don't have any equine tranquilizers on the property."

"Of course you do. Do you honestly think Lockie would be running a barn with twenty horses and have no way to tranquilize one in an emergency? Look in the tack room refrigerator. It's behind something else."

"Be serious! Call her."

"Talia, I'm busy."

The door opened.

"Leave Cam out of it," Lockie said and took the phone from me. "Hi. I'll be there in the morning. I'm leaving here before dawn."

"What?" I hadn't known it would be that early.

"I got a call a couple hours ago. Teche needs the jet," he said to me. "Yeah, I know," he said to Cam. "See you." He clicked off and handed me the phone. "Don't call him back."

"She needs him," I said.

"Let them work it out between themselves."

We left the pantry together and Jules regarded us with curiosity. No one else in the room cared because Adam Saunders was there in the flesh.

He was on, performing for the crowd, telling stories about what it was like on location in New Zealand. Of course he was charming, he was an actor. Acting isn't a job

198

for them, it's their life. Ryan was looking at him with absolute devotion and he wasn't responding in kind.

Cap glanced toward me and mouthed the words, "My dad."

According to her, attention hog didn't begin to describe her father. Instead of being properly embarrassed at his indiscretions, he went public. Cap and her mother had been humiliated when the entire country minus a few families who didn't have television sets, knew one family wasn't enough for him. There was a certain amount of pride, Cap insisted, that he was man enough for two.

He hadn't been a whole father for her, so Cap failed to see how he reached that conclusion but he did and she wanted nothing further to do with him.

I hoped that wasn't how Ryan was going to wind up. She wanted her father's approval so much and he wanted the adoration of the masses.

Or so it seemed to me after watching him in action for five minutes.

Motioning to Cap to follow us outside, I pulled Lockie out the door. "Let's find Greer, go to the I Screamery and have two scoops. We'll go away and maybe Adam Saunders will be gone by the time we get back."

"No," Lockie said. "I have horses to ride, and so do you. So does Greer. If we're going anywhere it's to the indoor." He headed to the barn.

I hurried to catch up to him. "Lockie?"

"Don't bring Cam into this."

"I understand your position but—"

"But ignore everything I just said and here's the important part," he replied.

"I understand your position AND I'm very concerned about Greer. Is that better?"

"If she's going to do something, let her do it. You can't protect Greer from herself."

"I don't want her to make a mistake while she's in emotional turmoil."

"You can't run after her, Tal. You can't be there every minute making life right for her. If she's going to do something, let her deal with the consequences."

"I disagree."

"I'm sure you do."

"Would it have been better for you if I left you alone and didn't make sure you went to Dr. Jarosz?"

He paused halfway to the barn. "I accepted your help. Greer doesn't want your help."

"She wants Cam's help!"

"You don't know that."

"I do. He reaches her in a way we can't."

"Then let them reach for each other on their own. Maybe what you want for them isn't what they want. This really is none of our business."

"If something came between us, there is nothing I wouldn't do to repair our relationship."

"You don't know that either."

"What could I learn that would make me behave contrary to my deepest beliefs?"

"I don't know, Talia. Life is like that. Suddenly it all falls down. Big shock. Your world changes in a moment."

I shook my head. "That's when you dig in." I continued on to the barn.

***

The rest of the afternoon was hardly harmonious and the horses were ridden in near silence. Greer had taken Joly and left the farm without saying goodbye or when she'd be back and the rest of us tried to make the most of the time we had with Lockie, even if he wasn't speaking to me. We finished the chores and returned to the house. Greer was nowhere in evidence.

Adam and Ryan were staying at the inn and having dinner with Victoria. It was just as well that Greer hadn't heard that snippet of Newbury News. I could only hope that Victoria would behave in front of a child but since she had never behaved in front of her own child, there was nothing that made Ryan any different. Except that Adam would be there and Victoria would want to make a good impression on him.

Having Cam in the *Tight Chaps* movie was fine, but Adam Saunders was a real get. He was a box office draw. Cam was a sexy nobody in comparison. Adam was a sexy somebody.

It was true, Adam was handsome, but he needed a shave, and didn't seem genuine. Lockie was far more handsome and exuded a reliability that couldn't be denied. Cam was very handsome, being blond never hurt anyone, and except for the last few weeks with my family, was always charmingly irrepressible.

If the choice was mine to make, I'd let Adam be in the darn movie and keep Cam where he wanted to be—with the horses. A movie would involve months away from riding and training. Adam had nothing better to do with his life from what I could tell. Cam did.

I didn't know what the future held for him or for Greer but I believed that he could reach her now. If someone could just be there to steady her until the turmoil ran its course.

Maybe Lockie was right and I was wrong. Leaving them to work it out for themselves could be for the best. But nothing would convince me that he wasn't the one to provide the stability she needed now. The harder she fought against it, the more certain I was. He was fifteen hundred miles away and wasn't planning on returning to Connecticut until next month. Greer would have to do this on her own.

A phone call once in a while from Cam. How would that hurt anything?

It would tell her someone outside the family was concerned about her.

That one small thing might have been all she had to hang onto. Because Greer felt we were all related so it was expected we would care. That didn't prove to her that she was worth caring about. If Cam cared about her, not what she could do for him or to him, that was what Greer needed.

When we finished the chores, Cap and I started for the house but Lockie held back so I stopped.

"I'm going to my house," he said.

"There's nothing there to eat," I replied.

"I'll find something in the freezer."

"I'll bring you something."

"Not necessary."

"Would you prefer being alone?"

"Let me know when you're going to start listening to me," Lockie replied and walked away.

I caught up with Cap.

"Since you were both shouting, I couldn't help overhearing," she said.

"I'm sorry."

"Shouting is part of it. Follow your instincts."

"What if I'm wrong?"

"What would be a better way to be wrong?"

We went into the kitchen where Jules was folding parchment paper over chicken breasts.

"Lockie doesn't feel well," I said. "What could I pack for his dinner?"

Jules explained how to bake the chicken in his oven, packed the risotto, the green beans, and beet salad in our picnic basket. I brought it to my truck, drove to the carriage house, and knocked on the door.

"Why are you knocking?" Lockie asked as he yanked the door open.

"Because it really is your house and I'm a guest. It's polite to knock. Maybe you're doing something and you would prefer not to be interrupted."

Lockie shook his head and returned to the desk where he was working on the farm bills.

Taking the food to the kitchen, I followed the instructions Jules had given me. While the chicken was baking, I set the table, not as well as Greer, but did my best with some apples and grapes in a bowl. After twenty minutes, I plated the food and brought it to the table then continued into the living room where Lockie was still working.

"Try to eat," I said.

"Try to trust me," he replied.

"What does that have to do with this?"

"You don't listen to me and you don't trust my judgment."

"About Greer and Cam?"

"Yes. There is a small chance I know more about it than you do."

"Lockie. I may know Greer better than you do."

"You do. I agree. However, you've never been in a relationship before. You've barely been out of Newbury. You haven't been exposed to a wide variety of people."

I stared at him. "The Briar School?"

"That's a homogenized population. They're all smart, they have the same aspirations, read the same books, thought the same thoughts. I taught at the County Day School in California. I know these kids."

"And you don't like them very much."

"It's a closed system. It has nothing to do with whether I like them or not. It's about what you learned about life by going there."

"This is more serious than I thought."

"Were you blaming this argument on a headache I was having?"

I didn't reply.

"That's a good answer. Yes."

He was right. Yes, I thought his irritability accounted for some of it and I still did. He didn't walk away from the accident with a bump on his head that two aspirins would cure, but that didn't mean what he felt could be dismissed.

"So you think I don't understand how relationships work because you're my first," I said.

"I think you are sensitive and compassionate and have the best of intentions. I know you want to help Greer. Extricating herself from the past is something she needs to do for herself."

"What do you think are appropriate ways I can help her?"

"Everything except bringing Cam into it."

I thought about it for a moment, then nodded. "Okay."

"What does that mean?"

"It means that I do trust your judgment and this is not the hill our relationship will die on." I turned back for the table. "Even if I know nothing about relationships."

"That's not what I meant."

"That is what you said."

"A man-woman relationship. It's different than family or friends."

"How? Not surface-wise, the anatomical, biological, physiological sex thing. The human interaction part."

Lockie pulled out the chair for me and gave me a nudge toward it.

"If you were not the first, in what ways would I be more clever dealing with you?"

Lockie sat across the table from me. "Phrased in that way, you appear to have won."

"But it's not about winning."

"No, it's about Cam. You only see a small slice of his life. There are other elements you don't know."

"That's true. Please eat before it's completely cold. Then we can spend the few hours we have left not thinking about Guy, the French Sausage Man."

"That's an image I didn't need in my head." Lockie opened the parchment and the chicken was still steaming.

After dinner, I helped him pack his clothes for Florida. There were several pairs of breeches, shirts, socks and such, as well as civilian clothing.

"I never asked before but what do you do in the evenings?"

Lockie zipped the bag closed. "There are always parties I don't attend."

"Do you go to dinner with friends?"

"Teche invites us quite often. People are interested in who is riding the winning horses, so Teche is able to show his horses off during the day and his riders at night. I pass as often as I can but it really is part of the job."

Counterpoint was doing well for a young horse with no experience at that level, but I was sorry Bittersweet Farm wasn't getting the interest, too. I was sure everyone was told Lockie was our trainer but most people had to think he rode for Acadiana and never heard of us. Teche loved the publicity but the Swope Foundation needed to have some public awareness, too. This was something I'd have to concentrate on during the season. My father, my family, deserved that effort. Greer was miles ahead of me with the Ambassador of Good Cheer.

I had a van painted in our stable colors and our name on it, and it was rarely moved out of the yard. That needed to change.

"Let's get into bed and watch some television," I suggested.

"Television and me, not such good friends," Lockie replied.

I went to the antique cabinet Victoria found, opened the drawer, and removing a DVD, waved it in the air. "Hugh Wiley's Nautical according to Walt Disney. *The Horse with the Flying Tail.*"

"Unless I'm mistaken, it's not a documentary."

"It's Walt Disney."

"So it's a Mickey Mouse production?"

"Yes. Mickey rides the horse while Minnie watches from the stands."

"What about that Pluto character? What was he?"

"A dog, I think. He was the groom."

"He licked the horse's coat instead of washing him?"

"That would result in one big hairball," I replied and paused. "I don't want to fight with you. I think it hurts you and I know it hurts me."

"Talia, we're going to argue. That's part of being in a relationship."

"No."

"Yes. As close as two people get, they are never one. Why would you want to be with your clone? Am I not a better companion?"

"Of course and I love how our differences draw us together but I don't want to fight with you."

"That's how it works. Go take your shower and we'll watch Mickey ride the palomino pony."

I put my arms around him. "Don't go back to Florida."

"Say it again next weekend and it'll be so," Lockie replied then kissed me.

14

"I'VE BEEN THINKING about the Zuckerlumpens," I said.

Under a gray and darkening sky, Greer and I had gotten to the farthest field before our silence was broken.

"Jules had this idea about Ryan transferring to Briar and keeping Ding here."

Greer shook her head. "How is that good for her?"

"She likes us."

"You can't buy a family even if Adam Saunders makes twenty million bucks a movie. The Swopes aren't for sale."

I looked at her.

"So your mother didn't use Dad's name, that doesn't make you less of a Swope."

"This is too much for me to handle all at the same time. If Ryan stayed here—"

"Then I have to take her to shows because the Zucklumpens are not triple A level. Aside from the fact that I thought the plan was that I would take the ponies to shows and you would stay home and train."

"There's too much showing going on. Once a month is enough."

"You're nuts. Adam Saunders isn't going to pay us two thousand dollars a month to babysit his daughter and not have her showing every weekend."

"She doesn't need that pressure."

"So you say."

"Because we've both been there."

"Just because you didn't like it doesn't mean that the pony hunter division isn't full of little girls who love showing every weekend. Rethink this plan."

I had thought enough. "I'd like to see Poppy on Ding and Ryan on Call."

"Did you have a nervous breakdown because Lockie left? Why should Adam Saunders buy Superstar Pony for his daughter to ride then let some 4-H'er ride him?"

"Because it would be good for his daughter."

"Don't you realize that's not the point?" Greer was exasperated with me. "You pay big bucks to win and have a photo in The Chronicle with a caption saying 'Ryan Saunders, daughter of film star Adam Saunders, and pony hunter champion Somebody or Other'."

"Greer, we can't do Bittersweet Farm like that. If that's the philosophy, then we should quit now. I couldn't live with myself if the horses didn't come first. I couldn't train kids to believe otherwise. We have to stand for something."

"We do." Greer turned her face to the sky. "Tal, you so often miss the obvious. For so many, it's not about sport, it's about emotional gratification."

It was starting to snow so we headed back to the barn.

***

While we were having lunch, Cap received a text message that Mill would be traveling north with the polo ponies within a few weeks. She was beyond happy so I didn't ask if that meant he would still be going to Europe for the summer as had been mentioned several weeks ago.Someone on the farm should be happy besides the ever-happy Jules.

As we were starting on dessert, Aly came to the door and we welcomed her in to join us.

"Half day at school because of the impending snowstorm," Aly said as she took a slice of torta al ciccolato, Jules's stellar chocolate cake with pastry cream between the two layers and fresh raspberries on top.

"More snow," I sighed.

"What I want to say is that this morning Adam dropped Ryan off at my house to finish out the rest of the week." Aly stirred milk into her tea. "She's at the barn with Poppy."

"Was it too much responsibility for him to stay with her during her vacation?" Greer asked. "Speaking as someone with plenty of experience of being off-loaded to anyone who would pretend to watch me when the school forced me out the door."

"He gave her a check to give me, like we were a B&B," Aly said as she took a forkful of cake. "This is so good!"

"Thank you," Jules replied.

"I didn't take Ryan in to be paid," Aly continued, then laughed. "Although there seems to be good money in it!"

"I'll help them get ready for their lesson," Cap said, pushing back from the table and bringing her plates to the sink.

I followed her out the door and we arrived at the barn to see the girls grooming their ponies.

"Good work," I said. "How about switching ponies today?"

Silence.

"When you say yes, we'll start the lesson."

"Yes," Poppy replied under duress.

"Of course she wants to ride my pony," Ryan said.

"Oh you mean the cheap pony who beat you at the show?"

"You wouldn't have beaten me if I had been on my WEF pony hunter champion," Ryan shot back.

"Your pony is so much nicer than you are," Poppy replied.

"There's no lesson with me today," I said. "I will not tolerate that kind of behavior in this barn."

Ryan burst into tears.

Poppy let her pony's hoof return to the floor. "I'm sorry, Talia. All she does is insult Tango."

"Ryan, come with me." I walked down the aisle and into Greer's office. After Ryan entered, I closed the door and handed her a tissue. "Okay. What's going on?"

"I don't want to ride her pony."

"Why not?" I waited for an answer. "Just spit it out. Say the words because we all know anyway."

"He's not as good as Ding."

"In what way?"

"Ding can win at an A rated show," Ryan said.

"And Tango Pirate can't?"

"That's right."

I sat on the edge of the desk. "Because he's gone to A rated shows and has lost to better ponies?"

"He would."

"But you don't know because Poppy has never taken him to a big show."

"He's a backyard pony. Ding is a show pony. My father bought him for me so I would be on the best."

"So you want to ride the best pony and be the best rider."

"Yes!" Ryan replied in delight that I finally got it.

"Why?"

"Because everyone wants to be the best."

"Not everyone."

"If you want people to treat you well, if you want to be special, then you have to be the best. That's what my father says. He knows. He's one of the top stars in Hollywood."

"If you're not the best, say you're second best, then what?"

"Then you're nobody," Ryan said.

"Invisible?"

"Exactly."

This was a tough burden for a little girl.

"I was brought up to believe that if you were kind and generous, that was better than winning ribbons," I said.

By Ryan's expression, I could tell that this was an alien philosophy to her.

I slid off the desk. "You've been blessed with so much more than most girls your age. Feel free to ride your pony in the indoor. You can finish up your week and we'll have Ding brought to Semple Hill Farm, okay?" I opened the door and took a step out.

"Talia, if I don't win, I will be invisible to my father," Ryan said softly.

She was invisible to him already. I thought she probably knew that already. What she didn't know was that Adam Saunders probably felt that if he stopped his tap dancing routine, he would become invisible, too.

"Be the best you, Ryan. That's harder than winning rosettes but you'll get more out of it."

On the aisle, Tango Pirate was ready to go. Wearing her helmet that looked like a bucket on her head, Poppy was kissing her pony. That was something I had never seen Ryan do and I didn't know how that instinct could be taught.

I watched them ride in the indoor for about twenty minutes until the snow started falling in earnest, then told them to call it a day. Aly still had to drive them home and the roads were going to get worse and not better as the afternoon went along.

There were still horses to be ridden. On the white board in the tack room, Cap had made a schedule template and every day I filled it in with who was supposed to ride whom. Freddi was set to ride Tyr and McStudly this afternoon. Cap would ride Spare and Bijou. I still had to ride Wing, Whiskey and Jetzt unless I could talk Greer into getting on Wing. She wouldn't get on one of Cam's horses, there was no sense in asking.

I put Whiskey on cross ties, and was getting my saddle when my phone rang.

"Hi."

"Hi. Is everything okay?" I hadn't heard from him since he left and he usually called when he arrived.

"Not exactly. Cam can't ride this weekend so I spent the most of the day working with him on Tropizienne and Tabiche so we'd be ready for the classics."

"It'll be fine."

"Cam's a good trainer. I won't have any problems."

"Did he get hurt?"

I didn't know what would keep Cam from riding, probably even a broken leg wouldn't do it.

"His grandfather is having some health issues and Cam wants to be there."

"It must be serious then."

"Serious enough but nothing he won't recover from so don't get yourself worked up about it. I don't know if Cam will have time to come by and see the horses or not."

"I can't not tell Greer."

If I wanted to keep what little trust she had in me, I had to tell her. She'd be watching Lockie ride Counterpoint over the weekend and couldn't help but see Cam wasn't riding.

"Okay. It's your decision."

Knowing Cam's propensity for ignoring the telephone, I doubted he would call ahead if he was going to come to the farm. It would be so much better to have a little heads up in order to avoid a confrontation.

"What would you do?"

"Tell her. They are both going to be at the farm. They can't avoid each other indefinitely."

"I think Greer could give it a good try."

"I would expect it of her. I have to go get on someone's horse, I don't remember their name. It's a hunter."

"I'll talk to you later."

"Bye, Tal."

"Bye." I hoped he heard that before he was gone but that chances were minimal.

I finished tacking up Whiskey and rode through the snow to the indoor to exercise him.

***

"Your grandparents were going to come home this afternoon," Jules said, "but the weather changed their minds. So it's just the three of us."

"Cap didn't say anything when she left for town that she wouldn't be coming back."

"She called and is staying in Old Newbury for the night."

Joly dashed in followed by Greer. "Are we getting that much snow?"

"The last weather report I saw said four inches," Jules replied.

"That's nothing. When we lived in Switzerland—"

"Wow!" I teased.

"Four inches wasn't noteworthy."

"It's enough to scare everyone here."

Jules checked on what was baking in the oven. "Now if I was back home, four inches would make international news."

"Did you ever see it snow in Los Angeles?"

"Yes, there were a few times flakes fell."

"Do you rush to get your sleds?" Greer asked.

"We didn't have sleds, we had surfboards. I suppose we could have used them if we turned them upside down."

"There are hills in Los Angeles. The observatory is on one."

"Griffith. Yes. Not very good for sledding, though. Where's your sled? We can use it tomorrow. It will be just like in the pictures. We can bundle up and wear ski caps and come in for hot chocolate. Brrr!"

Greer and I looked at each other.

"We didn't have a sled," she said.

"A toboggan?" Jules asked.

"You're teasing us now," I said.

"I am. You skied, of course."

"Of course," Greer replied.

I shook my head. "Dad doesn't ski."

"That's another thing my mother doesn't like about him. On the other hand, once she kicked him free, there were such cute ski instructors to play with."

"That is so true. In their off-season, they're male models," Jules agreed.

"Maybe that's her next book. *Tight Bindings and Tight Buns.*" I went to the table with the salad.

Greer and Jules laughed.

I hated to destroy that moment of happiness but it was best to break the news to her sooner rather than later. "Greer, Lockie called me and said he's riding for Cam this weekend."

"I know." Greer began to get Joly's food ready for him.

I couldn't respond for a moment. "How do you know?"

"Kate told me." Greer squirted salmon oil onto the food.

"Kate? As in Kate Rafferty Cooper, his mother?"

"That's the one."

"How did you happen to be talking to her?"

As far as I knew, the last time Greer had spoken to Kate Cooper was when we had both been to the house trying to track down Remington.

"I asked her to recommend someone in the area to do voice-over work for Good Cheer and she said she would. We've been talking ever since in order to get the project off the ground. I spoke with her just about every day this week because Kerwin hasn't been well."

Kerwin, now. She was calling Cam's grandfather by his first name.

"That's wonderful," I said, still in some disbelief.

Hours later when Lockie called to say goodnight, he couldn't believe it either.

15

THE MAJOR CLASSICS were scheduled for the weekend but Counterpoint had jumper classes on Friday and Lockie had two of Teche's young jumpers to ride in place of Cam. None of these were live-streamed so I had to depend largely on Tracy to call me with the progress and results. Lockie became very single-minded and focused when he was competing and most often didn't carry a cell phone with him, so I could only expect a call when the horses were back in the stalls.

Pavel cleared the driveway of what snow had fallen and we were working horses by mid-morning. Since Cap had the show in March coming up, she got on Spare and he was looking as fancy as I had ever seen him go. Bright and focused on his job, every stride showed his determination.

We started with some flat work to keep him flexible, then progressed to an S line exercise Lockie suggested. There were three fences set up to be ridden in an S configuration. The first jump was a curve to the right, the second fence was in the middle, and the third fence required a curve to the left. Eventually, the horse and rider would jump the combination in a straight line, although the fences would be taken at an angle.

Cap and Spare were a good team but they had the potential to be terrific because they trusted each other. The progress they'd made this month was very encouraging and I was beginning to look forward to what they would do in the spring shows.

There was a large A rated show Greer and I had gone to every year at the Miry Brook Hunt Club, which was a graceful, old establishment with striped awnings on the club house, large shade trees and lovely gardens. It was a show Lockie would want to do and now it seemed as though a good fit for Cap and Spare.

As much as I disliked showing, I had never minded going to Miry Brook because it was beautiful and a piece of history fading from the scene. It was possible to stroll through the trophy room where there were photos and silver bowls from nearly a hundred years ago. There were two rings, an outside course which they still used, and, of course, a polo field. The show committee managed to keep it from being highly commercialized. There were no jumps where the wings were in the shape of beer bottles, and no music blaring from the loudspeakers. It would not have been a surprise to see a group of riders appear from the main stable wearing pegged canary breeches.

After I raised the rails a hole, Cap and Spare took another pass through the gymnastic. He was light and responsive without being overly forward. I liked the expression on his face, the enthusiasm he had.

Spare wasn't a good horse for Greer. On paper it should have been the right team but maybe he just liked Cap better. Their personalities were in tune with each other.

Greer needed a horse, like Citabria, who could overlook the fact that she didn't always leave her emotions on the ground.

"That's good for today," I said. "How did he feel?"

Cap dropped the reins and gave him a big pat on the neck. "He always tries so hard to please." She paused. "I think we have to be careful about that."

"What do you mean?"

"We shouldn't give him too much to do, take advantage of that keenness."

I nodded as Cap dismounted.

"He's not going anywhere. He'll never be for sale. It's completely unimportant if he ever wins a class. Isn't that right?"

"Yes."

"We don't have to push him like other barns would."

"You belong here," I said as we walked out together.

"Me?" Cap smiled. "It's a good place to live."

"Yeah. Especially now that you don't have to sit on the ugliest couch in the world!"

***

After lunch, Aly arrived with Poppy and Gincy who ran to get their ponies.

"Where's Ryan?"

"I drove her back to the school. It was open and they were glad to have her. On the way, we stopped at Semple Hill and had a tour of the facility. It's beautiful and she should be very happy. It's not a large stable but the horses look excellent and Sideshow Ding will be in his element," Aly replied.

"It worked out then. I'm happy for them, and thank you for taking care of her."

"Ryan's...out of touch with reality and the only cure for that is a big dose of reality."

"Which her father can pay for her never to get."

We watched the girls twirl their pony's tails around.

"I feel sorry for Ding. He's a good guy."

"She'll outgrow him soon and he'll find himself with another little girl, hopefully one who will love him," Aly said.

"What are you going to do with Tango when Poppy outgrows him?" I asked.

"We can't afford two horses. We'll have to sell him."

"Think about letting us keep him. We'll find a ride for her and come out even."

"That sounds fine. That's the trouble with kids. They don't stay small!"

I liked Tango and wanted him to have a good home. Gincy had a younger sister who would take Beau over when the time came, so he wasn't a concern. Finding riders for Tango would never be a problem and no matter what Ryan thought, I did see a future at larger shows for him. He had that unusual dun color, a cute face, a nice stride, and was square over his fences. The fact that he didn't cost as much as a Ferrari didn't mean he couldn't win at an A show. Tango wouldn't be a sure thing and he might have trouble pinning over an expensive pony but I was sure he would never be an embarrassment.

My phone rang as the girls were warming up.

"Hi, Tal. It's Tracy."

"Hi. How is Bittersweet Farm South doing?"

"Lockie is on a roll. He just won the class on Counterpoint and about two hours ago took the class on Teche's horse, Maque Choux."

226

"Yippee! Counterpoint!"

"He's looking good. And Lockie is surrounded by so many people he can't get to his phone," Tracy said.

"What people?"

"Shark people. Whoever wins, there's a feeding frenzy. 'Ride my horse. Ride my horse.' They'll ditch their rider for someone they think can do a better job at getting the blue. It's crazy. I can't wait to get home."

"We miss you. Do you know when you're leaving?"

"I think Teche's first trailer leaves on Monday so there's no reason Counterpoint can't be on that, as far as I know."

"Terrific. Come home and take a week off. Go somewhere."

"I've been somewhere! And now I've got to go somewhere else. Lockie needs rescuing. I'll remind him to call you."

"Thanks, Tracy." I clicked off and turned back to the Zuckerlumpens. "Let's switch ponies."

The girls pulled their ponies to a halt and dismounted.

"Gee, I love you guys," I said.

"We love you, too, Talia," Poppy replied.

***

227

It was dark when I finally reached the house, smelling of horse, dirty and wet.

"Go get cleaned up, we're going out," Greer told me. "I already called Cap and told her."

"Why are we going out and can I just stay home?"

"Vico's been calling Jules all afternoon."

"Okay. Where are we going?" I asked heading for the stairs.

"That new Chinese place," Greer called after me.

I remembered the one she meant, Mu Dan. The one with real Chinese food, not take-out. As long as I wasn't served snake, I'd be fine.

Twenty minutes later, we were going out the door with the house phone ringing.

"What if it's someone important?" I asked.

"Anyone important has our cell numbers," Greer replied.

"Girls night out," Jules said as we got into the car and she headed for the restaurant.

Girls on the lam, it seemed to me, but the bizarre was becoming the norm so I was willing to go along with it. Vico still had the phone number and he could still call at midnight if he so chose. There was more between them than Jules had admitted, which was her right. She wasn't required to tell me the details of her life anymore than I revealed the details of mine. It was just if we needed Pavel to chase Vico away with the tractor one day, it would be good to know why.

The restaurant was lovely and the service was wonderful because we were just about the only people in there since the roads were icing over. Jules gave us a lesson in Chinese cuisine and chicken chow mein was still not on the menu. There were no fortune cookies for dessert. I missed that. Even if the fortune read "Rivers need springs" and I always said cars need springs.

We returned home, and I felt we were all missing someone but was smart enough not to say it.

It was nearly midnight when Lockie called.

"Hi, Tal. Sorry. I was out at a fancy dinner with Teche. Too loud. Too late. Too tired."

That meant he had a headache but I wasn't going to mention that either.

"So you're the hot new thing. I could have told them that."

"Was Greer happy about Counterpoint?"

"We were all pleased. I called Dad and he thought it was wonderful. He said to thank you for all your efforts."

"I think Counterpoint has a nice career in front of him and any time you want to sell him, he can be down the road in ten minutes."

"Sorry. Hotel Bittersweet. You can check in anytime you want but you will never leave."

"We can't collect them, Miss Margolin."

"I made an offer on Tango today."

"Good choice. He's a nice pony."

"Ryan left."

"I'm sorry it didn't work out better than that. She seemed like a nice kid."

Seemed was the operative word with the Saunders family.

"Go to sleep. You have a big day tomorrow and I'll be watching you," I said.

"Top riders, top horses. This isn't the usual catch ride."

"You're not the usual catch rider, Lockie and each class is one class closer to coming home."

"Have a good night, Silly."

"Good night, Lockie."

***

The next day, we all sat in the den with the television set up to show the streaming video of the Gator Classic. Jules made a large bowl of our favorite butter toffee popcorn but I was too nervous to eat. This wasn't like watching a movie for me. It was too real.

Lockie called me earlier to assure me that everything was fine. Tracy called several times after that to let us know what was happening.

There was big money involved so most of the top riders in the country had traveled to the show for the one class.

The fences were enormous, Tracy said, having walked the course with Lockie. She said some of them were nearly as tall as she was. The oxers were wider than they were tall.

I pulled the phone away from my ear and wondered if I should be listening to this. The fences looked big but did I need confirmation of that?

"How is Lockie?" I asked with each called.

"Fine. He doesn't seem the least bit nervous," Tracy reported.

At least one of us was relaxed.

Right on time, the class began. We watched twenty horses go before Tropizienne's name flashed on the scoreboard and Lockie entered the arena.

Jules patted my shoulder. "Buck up. It'll be over in two minutes."

The jumps looked worse than Tracy said, and the course was comprised of several difficult turns and a challenging combination that went down the diagonal into the sun. Several horses hit at least one rail, probably because they couldn't see it with the light in their eyes.

Not only did the horse and rider have to go clear, but they had to be fast. It was almost impossible to be both on this course.

Lockie began to canter Tropizienne slowly in a circle, almost as if it was a hunter class, then he turned for the first fence and they were galloping hard. The pace didn't let up

231

for the entire round, as Lockie turned inside the lines the previous riders had taken.

"Bold choice," the announcer said.

"He will have to dial it back for eight. That's a very difficult fence to take flat out," the commentator said.

I saw Lockie do a small jumper style half halt to get the horse to prepare himself and they flew over the fence landing and, without slowing, galloped for nine. They took the combination with the three oxers and finished the course with a five rail vertical.

Clear. Best time.

I could breathe again and left the room to take Joly for a walk.

Greer followed me. "He'll be alright."

I didn't reply as Joly ran ahead of us through the snow.

"It's not the same as the other time."

"No, it's not. That was deep mud and rain. Today it's clear and dry in Napier."

"It's hard to put the past in the past, isn't it," she said.

"Very. And it's not even my past."

"It reminds you of what you went through with your mother. Circumstances beyond anyone's control."

We walked in silence around the pond.

"It's difficult to believe there are situations Dad can't fix, isn't it?"

I nodded.

"That's life." Greer glanced at her watch. "I have to go."

"You're going? The class isn't over."

"If he wins or not, it's not the end of the world, is it?"

I watched her walked away then brought Joly into the house. By the time I got into the den, there were twelve more horses to go and no one had come close to Lockie's score.

The commentator was going berserk over it, in the way that these people lose all sense of proportion when describing sporting events. How could someone who didn't ride the circuit, come out of nowhere and catch ride a horse to the fastest clear time?

Apparently, there was no bio for Lockie available to the commentator because he didn't come out of nowhere. I felt uncomfortable having them discuss Lockie as though he was a dollar store horse.

Dollar store horses win championships without years of training. It happens in Walt Disney movies but very rarely in real life. They were acting as though Lockie was doing this without devoting most of his life to horses, riding and training. It would have been so simple to go back through the archives and discover he'd already ridden jumpers when he aged out of the junior division.

There was so much wrong in such a short amount of time.

After every horse had gone, there wasn't even a jump-off. Lockie had the fastest clear round. While we were waiting for the ceremony, there was a knock at the kitchen door.

I went to see who it was.

Cam.

I opened it. "Hi. I thought you were going home."

"I wanted to see the horses."

"Did you think you might run into Greer?"

"I have other things on my mind. Just wanted to let you know I was here. I think I'll get on Jetzt and see if you've gone backward with his training program."

"Cam. We've done everything we were instructed to do."

"Do you two girls have to be that sensitive?"

"Oh. Lockie just won the Gator Classic."

"On my horse?" Cam asked.

"Teche's horse."

"The one I've been riding and training for months."

"Come on and watch with us." I led him into the den. "Look who's here everyone."

Jules and Cap turned to Cam and froze.

"I can see how popular I am."

"I'm just surprised. Come sit next to me," Jules said. "They're going to do their beribboning now."

Lockie entered the arena riding Tropizienne who was wearing the winner's sheet. He posed for the photographer, holding up a trophy the size of a garden urn. They placed a large ribbon around the horse's neck and a sash type ribbon around Lockie.

He looked pleased. Teche stood there next to his horse, grinning. I was surprised he wasn't holding up the flaming Chartier Spice logo. Never let an opportunity for publicity go to waste.

Then it occurred to me that I needed to warn Greer not to come home.

While Cam watched the video replay of Lockie's round, I went into the kitchen to call Greer. It went to voice mail. "Hi. Call me before you come home," I said and clicked off.

My phone rang immediately.

"I'm so glad you got my message!"

"What message," Lockie asked.

"I thought it was Greer. We saw the class. It was fantastic. Congratulations. You were spectacular."

"You're not the only one who thinks so," he said.

"What?"

"I just had an offer to ride with the team in Europe this summer—"

The connection faded.

"With what team?"

Nothing.

"Lockie?"

No answer. I clicked off and tried calling him. It went to voice mail.

Now I really had to find Greer.

What offer had Lockie been given and would he want to take it? Would he want to spend the summer, and probably the spring away from Bittersweet?

I grabbed my jacket and ran to my truck.

Would he leave here? Was there an offer he couldn't turn down?

I jumped in my truck but didn't know where to go. "Think, Talia."

Where had Greer been going when she hadn't been around lately?

Putting the key in the ignition, I turned the truck on and started driving. About fifteen minutes later, I stopped in the Coopers' driveway, next to Greer's truck.

I got out, went to the door and knocked.

Kate answered it. "Hi."

"Greer's here, isn't she?"

Kate smiled and nodded.

"I really need to speak to her. I'm having a crisis of my own and, your son just arrived at the farm with no warning."

"He's a bad boy," Kate said then laughed as she ushered me inside. "Greer's in the sunroom with my father."

Kate led me through the house, then stopped before we reached the doorway. "Shhh."

Greer and Kerwin were sitting together on overstuffed furniture, the late afternoon sunlight streaming in, burnishing the scene. They were both smiling, books in their hands.

"She comes here and they read Shakespeare together. She has a real English accent and he doesn't but he tries. It reminds him of the career he once had. It makes him so happy to have the company. The audience." Kate laughed softly.

This was where she had been going when she was unaccounted for.

My sister became, in that moment, more precious to me than I could ever have imagined.

 The End

If you love a book, tell a friend.

Sign up for our mailing list and be among the first to know when the next Bittersweet Farm book is released. Send your email address to:
barbara@barbaramorgenroth.com

Note: All email addresses are strictly confidential and used only to notify of new releases.

About the Author

Barbara got her first horse, Country Squire, when she was eleven years old and considers herself lucky to have spent at least as much time on him as she did in the dirt. Next came Yankee Doodle who was far more cooperative and patient with her. Over the years, she showed in equitation classes, hunter classes, went on hunter paces, taught horseback riding at her stable called Sunshine Farm, and went fox hunting on an Appaloosa who would jump anything. With her Dutch Warmblood, Barbara began eventing and again found herself on a horse with great patience and who definitely taught her everything important she knows about horses.

Printed in Great Britain
by Amazon